One Mon and a Wake UP

One man's story of what it meant to be a PJ

By

Chuck Jackson

One Month, 20 Days, and a Wake Up

Self published – 2016 – by Charles (Chuck) Jackson

All rights reserved. No part of this book may be reproduced (except for inclusion in reviews), disseminated or utilized in any form or by any means, electronic or mechanical, including photocopying, recording, or in any information storage and retrieval system, or the Internet/World Wide Web with out written permission from the author.

This book is a work of fiction. Names, characters, places, and incidents are the product of the author's imagination or are used fictitiously. Any resemblance to actual events, locales, or persons, living or dead, is coincidental.

ISBN-13: 978-1979959414

Cover Design by Tutiana Villa (villadesign.net)

Table of Contents

Introduction v

United States Air Force Pararescue viii

Thoughts of a Pararescueman viii

Chapter One 1

Chapter Two 11

Chapter Three 25

Chapter Four 35

Chapter Five 49

Chapter Six 61

Chapter Seven 77

Chapter Eight 89

Chapter Nine 103

Chapter Ten 121

Chapter Eleven 137

Chapter Twelve 155

Chapter Thirteen 167

Chapter 14 185

Conclusion 197

Introduction

Have you ever looked at a blank piece of paper or computer screen and imagined, if written, what the words would say? I am not talking about the email to a friend, the memo to your boss, or the short story you always wanted to write. I am talking about words about yourself, your emotions, your experiences, and the individuals in your life.

Imagine you will take one small portion of your life and write about it. What if it was something you had harbored because much of it was too horrible or too revealing to discuss, let alone write about? How would you begin and what would you say?

I will take you, my reader, into the blank pages and fill it with four years of a man's life. These are years he would have just as soon forgotten, at least some of them. They are years that took him from immaturity, immersed him into the reality of adulthood. He forced himself him to make decisions he was ill equipped to make. They were years that shattered humanity, or what he thought was humane. Those years included chasing an ambition when achieved was to provide the self-esteem lacking in his life.

I want you to take a ride on those blank pages. We will fill them with words that portray those experiences, emotions, and the individuals who changed him. Much of those blank pages contained experiences he once hid. These details include the horrors of an indefensible war. This was a war where the commanders put their troops into reckless jeopardy to meet the political ambition of a few. This was a war where the heroes returned home in dishonor and shame. A price many heroes paid for with their lives because of the careless disregard for human life.

This man felt honor he served. However, he, like so many who served with him in Vietnam, kept this honor suppressed. You might ask why reveal all of this now. Did our political leaders learn their lesson from Vietnam? Just give a thought to the lives lost and put in jeopardy in Iraq and Afghanistan. The difference is, our men and women of those wars when they returned, we honored them. What we now know are the abandonments of the Vietnam

Veterans. Stories like the one filling these blank pages, we acknowledge and revere those lost Veterans.

This writing and most writing must start somewhere. We will begin at a place critical to this man and his story. The desire of the author is to bring purpose, validity, and honor to those portrayed in the writings.

United States Air Force Pararescue

Thoughts of a Pararescueman

I am that which others do not want to be. I chose to go where others fear and excel where they have failed.

I ask for nothing from those that will not give… and reluctantly accept the thought of eternal loneliness,… should I fail.

I have seen the face of death, felt the stinging cold of fear; I have realized the harsh reality of just what this job is all about. I enjoyed the sweet taste of victory and love, but those were just fleeting moments.

I have cried, pained and hoped, most of all, I have lived times others would say are best forgotten…But,

At least I will be able to say that I was proud of who and what I am and that in my heart and soul I will always be a "PJ"

<Unknown author>

Chapter One

In January 1966, I started my second semester at Iowa State University. I was in a dilemma since my grades for my first semester were just enough to keep me off academic probation. I was doing worse my second semester. It was after mid-term exams in March, I received a letter from the Selective Service Board. They warned me I could lose my student deferment.

As with high school, I found college a difficult challenge. I had little self-discipline to use my time to study. My focus was on my part-time job and my active social life. After work, instead of studying, I would go out with a buddy drinking beer. We would then cruise the streets looking for girls.

With the Vietnam War going on, there was an increase in the draft. The word was draftees into the Army had an 80 percent probability of going to Southeast Asia. They drafted a friend from high school. Now I was nervous I might be next. When I sought advice; it was consistent; I should quit work and study my butt off. To quit work meant I would need some financial help. I did not want to go to anyone, especially my parents. Student loans were almost non-existent.

Against all the advice, I decided to quit school and enlist in the Air Force. I requested and they granted a delayed enlistment. Now I wanted to salvage a few classes. I chose the Air Force thinking it would reduce my odds of going to Vietnam. Besides, I was an Air Force Brat and I was considering a career in the military, as my dad had.

I wrote my dad, who at the time was in Korea. I disappointed him when I quit school. However, he was proud I did the responsible thing in joining the military, especially during a war crisis.

* * *

June 15, 1966, I took a bus to Des Moines, Iowa. I checked into Fort Des Moines. It was the regional induction center for all the armed services. They sent me to a large building that many years ago had been a horse barn for the Army Calvary. It was a converted large open barracks facility.

Walking in through what used to be one of the barn doors, there was row after row of single bunks. Most had a bare mattress rolled up at the bottom of the bunk. It was late afternoon and there were at least 50 men, some lying around. While others occupied themselves in the recreation area at the back left of the huge open room. At the back right were the latrines and showers. The only wall in the building was the half wall separating the latrines from the sleeping area. The large posts reaching 20 feet to the roof created the division between the rows of bunks. There had been no money spent offering any privacy or making the facility comfortable. The facility was large enough to handle three hundred men.

The first two days I received my physical, mental aptitude test and gathering of general information. Once completed, I waited my turn to go to the Air Force's basic training facility. Other than when we went to the mess hall, we stayed in the large horse barn. The days were long and boring.

Five days later, they notified my group we would leave to go to Lackland Air Force Base (AFB). We arrived in San Antonio after 2 AM. We stayed in a waiting room until after 7 AM when a military bus took us to Lackland AFB.

From the moment my group stepped off the bus, our basic training began. We left any semblance of civilian life behind. Every waking hour they told us when to eat, shower, dress, use the bathroom, etc. If we did not comply, we had a drill sergeant up our butts and screaming in our ears. Any infraction, no matter how minor, they disciplined us. If an individual messed up, they would discipline the whole squad. Everyone got the message and we worked as a group.

My dad said basic training was to force the individual to accept complete authority. They discharged those who just could not comply or were screw-ups. They left classified as 'Other Than Honorable'.

I did well with basic training and I got into physical shape. I was at the top of my class and awarded a medal for marksmanship using the M-16.

After basic training, they promoted me to Airman 3rd Class (E-2). They sent me to Sheppard AFB in Wichita Falls, Texas, for Medical Helper School. At Sheppard, they treated as if we were still in basic training. The school provided a basic course in the medical fields. Again, I ranked in the top ten of my class.

They told us our achievement in training would give us an advantage in selecting our career field. In actuality, the career field was a supply and demand process by the Air Force. More than half of my basic training squad went to Medical Helper School at Sheppard AFB. Then the majority in the Medical Helper class went to Gunter AFB in Montgomery, Alabama for Dental Assistant or Dental Technician school.

They gave us a week to travel to Montgomery. Some elected to fly home for a few days while others went directly to Montgomery. I joined four other classmates traveling by train; we stopped for two days in New Orleans. While in Texas, alcohol wasn't served on the train. As soon as we crossed the Louisiana state line, the bar opened and we started drinking. We arrived in New Orleans drunk and we left two days later still drunk.

* * *

When we started Dental Assisting School, they didn't treat us as if we were still in basic training. We did not have to march to classes and there was not a drill sergeant yelling at us. It was almost as if I was back in college. They confined us to the base on evenings. However, weekends, we were free to go anywhere as long as we returned by midnight Sunday.

In my class, the majority of the students were Women of the Air Force (WAF). The instructors preyed on the small number of males to tease us for being in a female field. From the day, I started this school and through the years I worked as a dental assistant, I hated it. While in school I rarely studied and, so, I barely passed the exams.

Several of the women in my class caught my attention and one, in particular, seemed interested in me. Her name was Gene Wayne. Yes, they spelled Gene as a male. Before and after class she would talk to me even if only to ask a question. She and one of her girlfriends would come over and join my roommate and me for meals at the mess hall.

We had an Air Men's Club that included TV rooms, a pool table, a library area, and a bar with a dance floor. They didn't allow full-strength beer and hard liquor. But they served near beer, a low alcohol content beer. Gene would often meet me at the Air Men's

Club. She was easy to talk with and I enjoyed being in her company. We dated while at Gunther.

* * *

When we received our assignments, Gene, and I went back to Lackland AFB. I had two weeks to check in so I went to Ft. Worth to visit my mother. Gene went directly to Lackland.

I purchased a car in Ft. Worth and then drove the three hundred miles to San Antonio. They assigned Medical and Dental personnel to one of two areas. You either supported the large hospital (Wilford Hall) or the basic training operations. They assigned me to the latter.

I was on the base at least a month and I never ran into Gene. I asked about her but no one seemed to know who she was. It was also strange that I never ran into any of the other classmates from Gunter AFB. There was a mess hall right across from my clinic and I took most of my meals there.

A dentist requested I take files and dental impressions to the dental clinic next to Wilford Hall. When I found this rather large clinic, I took care of my assignment. Then I returned to the reception area and asked the Sergeant at the desk "Is there a Gene Wayne working here?"

"Yeah, there is. Would you like to speak to her?"

I could feel myself blushing, "Yes, if it isn't a problem."

The sergeant picked up the phone and after a short conversation, he said, "She is with a patient right now. If you can wait, she'll be out in a few minutes."

I waited and Gene came out smiling and looked pleased to see me. "Where have you been? I've been asking everyone if they had seen you."

I said, "I work over on the other side of the base. This is the first time I have been up in this area. I see Wilford Hall all the time, but I haven't come over here."

She asked and I accepted her invitation to have dinner with her at the hospital mess hall. After going through the line, we spotted two of our classmates from Gunter. We walked over and they invited us to sit with them. It was Paul and Kathy and they were now dating.

"Hey Ken," Paul said, "Where have you been?"

I said, "I work near the Green Monster. I've just never been to Wilford Hall." The Green Monster was a series of buildings attached in a large square. These buildings were for basic trainees to receive their uniforms. They did medical and dental exams, vaccine immunizations, and other administrative activities. As you might guess, the buildings were lime- green; however, in the Texas sun, they had faded. The area and the buildings were anything but attractive.

After dinner, I drove Gene to her barracks. We talked for two hours and I made a date with her for Saturday night. After our date, most nights I joined her for dinner at Wilford Hall. Our dating resumed and we enjoyed going to the base theater.

On weekends, we would drive around San Antonio exploring the city. Breckinridge Park was our favorite and we visited there often. The large park had plenty of picnic areas, nature trails, and botanical gardens. The main attraction was the zoo. There were open areas with Spanish Oak trees and lush grass where we could enjoy the outdoors.

* * *

From the beginning, I hated working at the dental clinic. The first dentist I worked with, Dr. Goldsmith, was right out of dental school. Dr. Goldsmith hated the military and resented having to work in this small clinic.

Dr. Goldsmith was always in a foul mood. If I did not give him the exact instruments he wanted, he would throw it on the floor. I would replace the instrument. Instead of telling me what he wanted, he would continue to throw the instruments until I got it right.

After putting up with this for weeks, I decided I would not put up with it any longer. I did not care if I got into trouble. Dr. Goldsmith was going to stop throwing instruments or get another assistant. The next day, Dr. Goldsmith had thrown at least five or six instruments. He put out his hand expecting me to hand him another one. I did not respond. Dr. Goldsmith said, "Where in the hell is my carver?"

I said, "I have no more; you threw them all on the floor."

I got up and left the room. I could hear Dr. Goldsmith screaming, "Airman Johnson, get your ass back in here."

After finishing his patient, Dr. Goldsmith went straight to Sergeant McInnis, my supervisor. Sgt. McInnis called me in to explain my actions. I told Sergeant McInnis about Dr. Goldsmith throwing instruments. Sergeant McInnis chuckled, "I wondered how long you would last. You are the fourth assistant he has had in eight months. I will go talk to the Colonel again about his behavior. For now, let him work by himself." He reassigned me to work in the dental surgery area.

Sergeant McInnis was a Chief-Master Sergeant, easy going, and rarely lost his temper. He reminded me of my dad, with the steel blue eyes and thick white hair. As with my dad, I could tell when he was teasing, his eyes would twinkle. I was fond of Sergeant McInnis and respected him. He took a liking to me and became my mentor.

I often went to Sergeant McInnis complaining about having to work as a dental assistant. I would beg him to find me a cross-training opportunity. He became tired of my whining and he sent me over to the Green Monster. I worked charting teeth on basic trainees' records and taking and developing x-rays. If I was not busy, I helped over in the medical area. I took blood pressures, height, weight, etc. On other days, I gave vaccinations using an air gun apparatus. With these guns, four medics could vaccinate a squad of a hundred men in less than fifteen minutes. It was like running cattle through a chute. If we had an individual faint, we moved him over to the side and continued shooting the others. We were to speak and treat the basic troops harshly, giving no regard to their feelings.

I tolerated working at the Green Monster for six months; however, they sent me back to the same dental clinic. Once back, I learned how to do dental cleanings and patient preventative care. It was something new and challenging. After a couple months, I became disinterested. I was back complaining to Sergeant McInnis.

When I told Sergeant McInnis about my dad, he said the name sounded familiar. He thought they might have been stationed together in the past. It was months later that my dad said he remembered Sergeant McInnis. My dad was on the enlisted men's review board for promotions at Sioux City AFB. He was instrumental in Sergeant McInnis' promotion to Master Sergeant.

Sergeant McInnis seemed to look out for me and tried his best to keep me out of trouble. Sergeant McInnis retired a year after my dad. I thought it was ironic that Sergeant McInnis crossed both my dad and my paths

Chapter Two

In April 1967, Sergeant McInnis told me about a cross-training opportunity, if I could qualify. They would send me to Special Forces training for Pararescue. You had to pass a rigorous physical fitness assessment and physical exam. They didn't give me any details on the physical fitness assessment, other than only one out of ten passed. With my confidence high, I went to the squadron personnel office and submitted my application.

I learned all armed services have Special Forces. The Army has the Rangers and Green Berets, the Navy, and Marines the Seals, and the Air Force Pararescue. Pararescue is a medically trained team whose duties included search and rescue for down pilots.

Although determined to do what it took, it concerned me I might not be physically fit enough to meet the requirements. Every day, I would do as many sit-ups, push-ups, and other calisthenics until I could not do anymore. Then I would go out running, increasing my distance each day. I quit smoking knowing it would assist in my endurance and strength. They did not give me a specific date for testing, but the personnel office estimated I had six weeks to prepare.

Five weeks after applying, they notified me I was to report for testing the following Monday at 0900. I arrived early at the old base gymnasium, which was a few blocks from the Green Monster and checked in. There were about 50 Airmen sitting in the bleachers waiting for the unknown procedures to begin. The majority was still in basic training while a few as me had at least one stripe on our fatigues. There was even a Staff sergeant, although, he looked overweight and out of shape compared to the young men going through basic training.

At exactly 0915, a Master sergeant dressed in starched fatigues with his pants bloused and tucked into his spit-shined jump boots and wearing a burgundy beret walked through the door. All heads shifted to watch this impressive looking man enter. He stepped to a podium and introduced himself. He said, "I am Sergeant Kelly, NCOIC (non-commissioned officer in charge) of this training program. For some of you, this will begin a rewarding experience and perhaps a career in the Air Force. However, most of you will have a short day and will return to your squadrons. I am not here to blow smoke up your butt, we only accept those men who have the drive and determination to push yourself further than you have ever gone." There were a moan and a nervous shifting on the bleachers.

He continued telling us a brief history of Aerospace Rescue and Recovery Squadron (ARRS; e.g. Pararescue). He said, "We train you to go anywhere in the world to get people out of predicaments they may or may not have created. We rescue them and keep them alive. We train you to recover these individuals by parachute, SCUBA, helicopter, or good old 'shoe leather'. Whatever it takes or where ever we have to go; jungle, desert, mountain, or ocean, it is our job to pull their butts out and save their lives. Our most essential skills are in our medical training. All the other training is for us to get in and get out alive. Simply put, our motto is *'We Do This, That Others May Live'*. We are known within the Special Forces as PJs or Para jumpers."

He continued, "Shortly we will give you physical tasks to complete. Anytime during the day, you cannot complete the required task, you will be eliminated. If you decide this is not for you, return to the gym, shower, and return to your squadron." He then instructed us we would have five minutes and not a second more to change into our PT clothing (military issued shorts, tee-shirts, and boots), and fall into formation outside the front doors of the gym. We still did not have a clue what physical demands were ahead of us.

He looked us over; reached into his pocket to retrieve a whistle and a stopwatch. We heard the shrill sound of the whistle and there was a loud rumble as all 50 plus men headed for the locker room to change. There was not one man who did not make the formation in the allotted time. Sergeant Kelley and three other sergeants dressed in PT clothing met us out front. We marched in formation over to an adjacent athletic field where we warmed up with calisthenics. Surrounding the athletic field was a half-mile track and they required us to complete an untimed four-mile run. Although this was South Texas, the weather this day was in the low sixties, windy, and as we were warming up, it poured rain. I watched as the instructors conferred and gave each other a cynical smile. I knew then, this would be brutal.

The track was nothing more than a dirt path, with potholes, rocks, and uneven bumps. The rain made it a mire of water and mud. When I had run my first mile, I was soaked, muscles straining from the cold and my wet boots felt like lead weights. I watched after mile three, one man after another fall to the wayside. By the time, I finished my run, at least a dozen men had dropped out.

They gave us a ten-minute break and then reassembled over near the gym by a series of pull-up bars. I thought this is when they will eliminate me. In high school PT and sports, anytime we had to do chin-ups, I had difficulty. One of the training sergeants demonstrated the correct and the wrong way of doing chin-ups. The bar was at a height you had to jump to grab it. The sergeant said, "You will let your arms fully extend and hold until I tell you to begin. There will be no swinging or other movements to make this easier; you will keep your body straight. Once you complete your pull with your chin above the bar, you will return to the full extension of your arm, sound off with the completed pull. Heads and bodies not held straight, chins not above the bar, arms not fully extended; the pull will not count. At any time your feet touch the ground, you are eliminated. We require you to do four correct pulls with no time limit." There was a low murmur as we listened to the instruction.

One man asked if we could have a towel to dry the bar. I watched as the sergeant smiled, then laughed. "Do you think you will have a towel to dry things off when you are in the monsoon rains in 'Nam'? Get real, Airman."

When it came my time and after I completed my first pull, my arms, shoulders, and chest muscles were on fire. Silently I screamed at myself, *You will not quit — You will not quit*. I was so engrossed; I had not realized I had completed my fourth pull. I heard the sergeant say, "You are done, Airman. Unless you want to show off by showing how many reps you can do, get down." He did not have to say it twice.

When we completed this part, our numbers had shrunk to twenty-five. They gave us another break. Back in formation, we marched in the continued cold rain to the base pool. We removed our wet boots, and socks, and they gave us the option to leave on our tee shirts. I knew the water would be cold and I opted to leave mine on thinking it would help keep my body warm. In hindsight, the wet tee shirt was a hindrance to my swimming.

The pool was Olympic size, twenty-five meters, and we were to complete five hundred meters. The training sergeant said, "You can use any stroke you want. Again, there is no time limit on your swim. I warn you, we will watch and anytime you touch the bottom or the side of the pool, you will be eliminated. Do not feel ashamed to ask for help to get out when you complete your swim or if you cannot complete it. I will really be pissed if I have to pull your sorry ass out from the bottom of the pool." No one was laughing.

I was a fair swimmer, but my endurance had always been poor because I found it difficult to relax in the water. When I was Boy Scouts, I received a merit badge for swimming five hundred meters. However, it was eight years and I had not been smoking.

There were four swimmers in the water at one time and I was in the second group. To complete my swim, I would turn on my back and just kick with my legs; I even dogged paddled to give my body recovery. Again, I was yelling at myself to not give up for the last few laps. I also kept thinking about how much I hated dental assisting.

When we completed our swim task, our numbers were now 15. We lost 70 percent; Sergeant Kelley had predicted 80 percent. Of the fifteen, only three of us were not in basic training. I was drained of energy, however, as we marched back to the gymnasium, I felt elated I was among the survivors.

After a hot shower, we dressed and met back at the same spot we began the day. As we slumped in the bleachers from exhaustion, Sergeant Kelley addressed us at the podium. He said, "Later in the week we will contact you for your physical exam appointment at Wilford Hall Hospital. Failure to show up or tardy, you will be eliminated from the program. Gentlemen, do not get a big head because you made it this far. The pre-training school is just beginning. You are to report to the ARRS Training classroom at 0800 next Monday to further determine if you have what it takes to be a PJ—Dismissed."

I dragged my butt over to my car to head back to the barracks. One airman not in basic training asked for a ride to the barracks. He was assigned to Wilford Hall and his barracks was next to mine. Back at the barracks, I threw myself down on my bunk and set my alarm so I would not be late for dinner with Gene at the hospital.

*　*　*

On Thursday, I had my physical and I had no physical discrepancies, which would prevent me from being accepted into the program. I notified my squadron personnel office I was entering the training program and they relieved me of my normal duties. Since they told us the physical strength assessment would continue, I resumed my setup, push-ups, and runs. There was a metal bar between commode cubicles in our latrine; I used it to do chin-ups.

On Monday, we met with Master Sergeant John Kelley, at the ARRS training offices and classrooms on the opposite side of Lackland from where I worked. The told us we would join a previous group of ten trainees. We would begin a five-week physical training and assessment period. It would also determine if we were suitable for entering the actual PJ training program or what they called the Pipeline.

It upset me when they told me I would move into the barracks with the basic trainees. It further upset me when he told us; they required us to set up a footlocker and clothing rack as we did in basic training. He said, "We will have periodic inspections, like basic training, only more stringent. There is a pull-up bar outside the door of the barracks and each time you enter or exit the barracks, you will do twenty-five pushups and eight pull-ups. We double time in formation everywhere we go. We will require you to run five miles in the morning and afternoon. Failure to do this daily or cheating by shortening your run will result in elimination from the program. We suggest you do your runs in small groups. Understand?"

"Yes, Sergeant," we replied in unison, sighed, and continued to listen to his detailed instruction.

"There is PT in the morning after your run. We swim in the afternoon. If it makes you feel any better, we don't expect you to do all this the first day or even the first week. Yet, we will evaluate you, and expect you to progress to meet certain goals. Failure to meet these goals or we see you aren't pushing yourself, you are out of the program." He paused a moment to let all of this sink in. "You will find to succeed in this training, you need to work as a team. Anyone who thinks they can tough it out alone will find themselves on a bus back to their squadron."

When Sergeant Kelley finished, he allowed questions. The training sounded so mysterious and apprehensive. During his briefing, he explained previous Pararescue training took eighteen months to two years to complete. Due to the escalation of the Vietnam War, the Pentagon had ordered increased numbers of trained personnel and the training time reduced. They told us we would go through the same training, although, it would be only fourteen months.

The other two non-basic trainees and I were given until 1600 hours to pack our duffle bags from the list of required uniforms, and personal items allowed, and report to our assigned barracks. The basic trainees came with their bags; they double-timed in formation over to our new barracks.

Before returning to my barracks to pack, I drove over to Gene's dental clinic to talk with her. Gene agreed with me it was ridiculous to be required to return to what I felt was more basic training. I was wrong; it was not anything like basic, it was more grueling. She objected when she would not see me during the week. I assumed I would have the weekends off, and I could spend them with her. I assumed wrong; the training continued weekends.

I returned to my barracks, packed my duffle bag with the required items. They told me to leave my car parked at my barracks. There was not insufficient space to park it, nor would they allow me to use it. I left the keys to my car along with a note for my roommate to drive it to keep the battery charged. I also told him I did not know when I would return.

Since no one was around to drive me, I caught the base bus over to the ARRS training center. While riding, I questioned myself if I was doing the right thing; however, the thought of returning to dental assisting pushed those thoughts from my mind.

When I arrived and walked into my new barracks, the Airman I had given a ride was standing just inside the door talking to another trainee. He said, "Hey, Johnson. Glad you could make it." I gave him a questionable look, then looked at my watch and realized it was after 1530 hours.

"Oh shit, I barely made it."

The other man said, "I'm Tommy Carpenter; I'm the class leader," he reached over and shook hands. "You better get your gear stored and be ready to fall in by 1630 for roll call and chow. Douglas, go help Johnson get settled."

Douglas introduced himself again, "Hey, I'm James Douglas. My friends call me Jimmy. Follow me upstairs, there is an open bunk next to mine."

We went upstairs, Jimmy helped me unpack, and get my things stored in my footlocker and open rack behind the bed. As we were getting my things organized, more men entered the barracks. Some I recognized from the previous week, but all of them were in PT gear and sweaty. They stripped, grabbed a towel, and headed for the showers.

As we were finishing, I heard Carpenter yell, ten minutes to formation. I followed Jimmy down the stairs and as we exited the door, one of the training sergeants was standing on the sidewalk. He gave us a look and said, "Johnson, Douglas; this your first day?"

"Yes, Sergeant," we said in unison.

"Okay, give me fifteen and four."

I remembered Sergeant Kelley's briefing, and I dropped in the grass and started my fifteen pushups. When finished I looked for the pull-up bar and found it next to the training sergeant. Jimmy was already on one and I jumped up on the other. I was struggling on my third one and I did not get down before I started back up. The sergeant yelled, "Johnson, that one does not count. You didn't fully extend. Give me two more." I strained but gave him two correct ones.

I moved over by Jimmy and we watched as the other trainees came out of the barracks, did their push-ups and pull-ups. Before they finished, they shouted and did three more, "One for the Air Force, One for Master Sergeant Kelley, and One for Pararescue." When everyone finished, the squad of twenty-five trainees, we double-timed in formation over to the mess hall. Just like basic training, you could not leisurely eat your meal; you quickly ate, took your tray to the kitchen window, and then hurried outside to join the others in formation. Again, we double-timed back to the barracks.

* * *

The days of continued assessment or as the instructors called it, Pre-training phase started each morning at 0600. We doubled timed it over to the mess hall and back. Given a few minutes to use the latrines and get dressed in our PT clothing. Then it was off for your five-mile run. We reassembled at the athletic field and started our physically crushing series of push-ups, sit-ups, flutter kicks, and whatever else the instructor threw at us. When we thought we were through, we started all over. It was obvious they wanted the individuals unable to keep up or those not willing to push themselves to drop out.

We double-timed to the mess hall for lunch and then over to the pool facility by 1300. Each day they increased the length we swam, shortened the rest periods, and increased the harassment. More trainees dropped out from this than anything else. It seemed they put more emphasis on the strength and endurance at the pool. I questioned it at the time; however, it became obvious months later in our training.

Even when exhausted from our workout at the pool, we concluded out physical training by running our second five-mile run. Back to the barracks, hit the showers, dress in starched fatigues, and we assembled for chow. Evenings we spent, getting our barracks, lockers, and uniforms ready for inspections. Inspections were, first thing in the morning or when we returned from our evening meals.

They laundered our fatigues with heavy starch daily. We kept our issued jump boot spit shinned each evening. When wearing our fatigues, we bloused and tucked them into our jump boots. They didn't require it, but most men, including myself, had our hair buzzed.

After two weeks, the group ahead of us, who were now eight, left Lackland and headed for the 'Pipeline', or the actual beginning of the PJ training. Our group was down to twelve. The next week, they shortened the PT and swim period and substituted this time with field training. This included wall climbing, rope swinging, belly crawls, etc. We had done this in basic training, but not daily.

A week later, another group of twenty men joined us and we returned to the killing calisthenics and swimming. At the end of the fifth week for our group of twelve, the Airmen in basic training graduated and they sent them into the Pipeline. They gave them two weeks before having to report. They sent the other two and I back to our squadrons and the told us we would get our orders soon. A week later, they notified me to report Fort Benning, Georgia for Airborne School (i.e. Jump or Parachute school). Now the twelve men who remained were moving into the Pipeline and they identified us as Class 67-4.

Chapter Three

I joined the other two Airmen stationed at Lackland, and we flew military standby to Atlanta. The third Airman was Robert (Bob) Thorpe, and he was a cook working at one of the basic trainee mess halls. Bob was like me, hated what he did, and was eager to cross train. Jimmy volunteered because he thought it would be "neat to be a PJ". He never complained, but I often wondered how 'neat' he thought it was when we were working our butts off.

Once in Atlanta, we met other military men, most Army, and they transported us by an Army bus to Fort Benning. This was an old Army Post and much of the facilities used for training were over twenty years old. As it was at Lackland, the barracks were two-story open bay.

Our school would be six to seven weeks. It would start with physical training, hand-to-hand combat, and weapons training. The final three weeks were Airborne or jump school. Our class, 67-4, joined trainees from the Army, Navy, and Marines. We now numbered over 50.

Jimmy took the bunk above mine. He was from Houston and had enlisted a few months after I did. Since we both claimed Texas as home, we became friends. Our friendship grew as we went through the Pipeline. It continued the years we served in the military.

Jimmy was shorter and smaller built than I was. He was in better shape than me. From the beginning at Lackland, he helped me with my physical training. Before I left Fort Benning, I could keep up with him and most men in our group.

With the co-mingled men of all the branches of the military, the Air Force trainees were the minority. The Sergeant who was in charge of our class was a well-trained and experienced Army Ranger. He said, "If you think this training is tough, wait until you get to Nam. You will thank me for getting you in shape." He was right.

While at Fort Benning, our look did not differ from other training units. Yet, we were identifiable as Special Forces because we double-timed instead of marched. The day began at 5 AM with a five-mile run. Classroom training was always after breakfast and lunch. Between, we were out in the field with combat or physical training.

The first week of jump school, was "Ground Week". It included more intense physical training. We learned when we would jump how to land without breaking our necks. We simulated hooking up and exiting the aircraft. We jumped off a four-foot platform landing with our legs flexed. You push backward to take the impact with our butts. We learned how to get into and adjust the harness apparatus we would use.

Week 2 was "Tower Week" and used two towers, one thirty feet, the other 100. We jumped from the lower tower, and by the end of the week, we were using the higher.

The day we started up the lower tower for the first time, I looked over at Jimmy, "Now this will be fun."

Once we reached to top, Jimmy said, "I'm not so sure Johnson. It's a hell of a long way to be jumping."

They gave us helmets and we wore a body harness with a strap and a snap hook on the end. When you took your turn, you attached the snap hook to a cable apparatus descending to the ground. The angle of the cable determined the speed and we were to land as they had taught us in week one. At first, the angle of the cable was wide and our decent was not fast. Each day the angle got steeper, and our speed increased.

I was never one bothered by heights. However, I was in fear when I stood on the edge of the platform and then pushing off. My heart would pound faster as I got closer to my turn to jump. As soon as I was on the ground, I was fine. I never adapted to tower jumping throughout the time we trained.

We moved to the one-hundred-foot tower, and we did the same thing with the cable. Then we wore parachutes. We still used the cable, but our parachutes would deploy and slow our speed of decent. Then, we jumped off the one-hundred-foot tower with just our parachutes.

The first time we used the parachutes, I told Jimmy, "Now this is much easier."

He half smiled, "Johnson, you're full of crap. What are you going to do if your chute doesn't open?" We laughed at each other and did our next jump.

Once on the ground, Jimmy asked, "Now Johnson, what do you think?"

I would always reply, "Piece of cake." Yet, I would sweat just like the rest.

The last week before graduation was "Jump Week". We boarded a C-130 aircraft for our first actual jump. The turboprop plane was the type where the rear section dropped for cargo loading. In our case, we walked the ramps and jumped from the rear opening. As the plane lifted off the runway, it was unforgettable observing the other trainees. We were sitting in sling seats along the outside walls. Some sat somberly with no emotions. Others had a look, as this was their last day on earth. Some, like me, got talkative and giddy to overcome the fear. Jimmy sat opposite me and I watched him turn red, then white, then green before he puked. I pointed my finger letting him know he would not get away with it without me teasing the hell out of him.

The time came for our jump, and the rear door opened. We stood, hooked our static lines with the snap hook on a cable above our heads. I was halfway into the aircraft and I watched man after man get to the end and make their jump. No one spoke due to the roar of the engines and the wind. The wind was so strong as you moved towards the end, the harder it was to keep your balance. For your turn, you leaned forward and just fell out. They gave a few a boot in the butt to encourage them to jump.

While I waited, I surprised myself. The increased heartbeat and the sweats I experienced with the towers did not happen. I felt confident, and I did not get scared. When my turn came, I looked the instructor in the eye. He gave me the signal, I leaned out, and the wind lifted me away from the aircraft. The chute activated, but it took several seconds to open. Those seconds took forever as I fell.

Even with the chute open, it looked like I was falling fast. Our instructors warned us of the sensation. They told us we would fall slower than the speeds we experienced from the towers. As we got closer to the earth, there was a false sensation as if we slowed. Then in the final seconds, the earth rushed up to you rather than you moving towards it. It came so fast I barely got my legs and body in the position for landing. The landing was a jolt, but again not any more than when we jumped off the towers.

As I got up, I felt the rush of adrenaline while gathering my chute. Before I knew it, nausea overtook me, and I was on my knees puking. As I lifted myself back up, I looked around to see if anyone had seen me, I spotted Jimmy fifty yards away. He was pointing at me and laughing his head off. Well, how was I going to tease him now? I did later tell him, "At least I didn't puke all over the plane."

That afternoon, we duplicated our jump from the same altitude. Perhaps it was because I knew what to expect, by the time, it was my turn to jump, my uniform was soaking from sweat. Yet, once out of the aircraft, I enjoyed the ride.

The next day, we went up again at a higher altitude. When the rear door opened, I felt the aircraft de-pressurize. Everyone looked more relaxed this time. We still had one or two men they encouraged to leave the plane

It had to be the higher altitude when I jumped the force of the wind and the chute deployed harsher. As with the second jump, the ride was enjoyable, and the landing was uneventful. Again, we did a second jump after lunch. After landing and finding Jimmy, I said, "This is a piece of Cake. What is so hard about this?" I don't think I fooled him, I was glad this was our last jump. I wondered if it would get easier when we jumped on a rescue mission.

The following day, after our five-mile run and breakfast, we returned to our barracks. We showered and dressed in our Class A uniforms. We double-timed over to the parade grounds for a graduation ceremony. They pinned each of us with our jump wings.

They were silver and a pair of eagle-like wings with a small parachute mounted in the center. In the Air Force, we wore our wings above the left breast pocket and an inch above our ribbons. These wings indicated we were men of the Armed Forces who qualified to parachute into combat. We wore our wings with pride.

That evening, Jimmy, Bob, and I had a flight to San Antonio. We returned to the barracks, packed, and caught a bus to the Atlanta airport. We had several hours until our flight so we sat around drinking beer and waiting. With an extended stopover in Dallas, it was the next morning we arrived in San Antonio.

That evening I met Gene at the hospital mess hall for dinner. I asked Jimmy to join me so he could meet Gene. Afterwards, we got a beer, went to the squadron patio area to celebrate. As we drank, Gene was gracious by listening to us brag about all the things we had done.

They told us at Fort Benning, we should get our orders to go to survival school. A week after I returned from Ft. Benning, they promoted me to Airman Second Class (E-3). Although I had to return to the dental clinic, Sergeant McInnis assigned me to the front desk.

* * *

One weekend, Gene and I were hanging out at a shopping mall. We were just walking around doing window-shopping. We stopped at a Zale's Jewelry Store and we were looking at wedding rings in the window. I teased her what our family and friends would say if we were to get married. I said, "Hey, just for fun, let's go in, and see what it costs for an engagement ring for you."

Her face flushed. "No," she said. "You can't afford it now."

"Come on," I said, "Let's do it for fun. I would like to know what type of ring you like and don't like."

Again, she gave me a look. "Okay, but we are doing this for fun, right?"

As we entered the store, I lied, "Of course."

I found Gene so easy to be with, it was natural we should be together. I didn't know if I loved her. I knew she was the only person I could confide my personal feelings of fear, confidence, and happiness. I felt if I did not move forward in our relationship, I might lose her.

Reflecting, I do not think I was fooling her, yet I thought I caught her off guard. She rejected any expensive rings. Yet, I could tell from her expression the style she liked. After a few minutes, Gene narrowed her search to two rings. One she liked had a larger diamond. The other had a smaller stone, although, Gene kept looking at the first. I pointed to it and asked, "What size stone is this?"

The sales clerk said, "It is over a half karat. If you like, we could put a smaller stone in it and it would be in the same price range as the other one." I wanted to hug the man. He had read Gene just as I had.

I winked at Gene and said, "Why don't you look around more and see if something else you like is better." She took the bait and walked away. I turned to the salesclerk, "What evenings are you opened late?"

"We are open on Thursday and Saturday nights."

Will you be here next Thursday?"

"Yes," he said smiling at me.

"Okay. I'll try to be back here next Thursday after work. I want to buy her the ring for Christmas." I thanked him and then joined Gene.

"Now, wasn't that fun?"

I could tell she was not buying my game. She smiled and said, "Okay, you had your fun. Let's get the hell out of here."

With my promotion, my pay doubled and I intended on buying the ring.

On Thursday, I returned to Zale's. The salesclerk discounted the ring with the larger stone. He told me if I would put it on credit with the store, the matching wedding ring would come with it at no extra cost. I filled out the application and left hoping they would approve my credit.

The following Saturday, I put a down payment on the rings and signed the credit contract. They agreed to hold the ring in their safe until I was ready to give it to her at Christmas.

* * *

When Jimmy and I did not get orders for our next Pipeline School in three weeks, we got apprehensive. Why were they delaying? One afternoon we went over to the ARRS School to talk with Sergeant Kelley. He attempted to calm our anxiety. He promised he would check into it and get back to us. Two weeks later, we received our orders. We were to report to Fairchild AFB for our next Pipeline training, survival school.

Chapter Four

When I received my orders for survival school at Fairchild AFB in Spokane, Washington, I was excited yet apprehensive. The Air Force's ARRS trainers would run this school, and the scuttlebutt was they would push us hard. You knew we would lose more trainees; I hoped I was not one of them.

When I told Gene I would leave the following week, she got upset. "You just got back."

"I don't think they care." Gene and I had never discussed what lay ahead after my PJ training. I was reluctant to tell her once I finished school, I would go to Vietnam. I wondered if she knew, would she marry me. I also questioned if she accepted, would we have time to get married between or after my training?

What seemed insignificant was the fear I previously had about going to Vietnam. However, I wondered how I would react the first time someone shot at me. Death was nothing I had given serious consideration, and I tried my best to abandon it now.

Once we arrived at Fairchild, the new barracks they assigned us were like dorm rooms with double occupancy, and a private bathroom. Jimmy and I shared a room. Class 67-4 joined another class of the same size.

As before, we started our day off early (0600 hours) with a five-mile run. The first week, we were back to our aggressive PT and pool routine. They wanted to make sure we had not slipped in our physical fitness. As always, we double-timed in formation anywhere we went. The second week they familiarized us with the helicopters would be using. They allowed us to become accustomed to being around them, and then we simulated rescue operations.

As a teen, I had taken a ride on a helicopter to tour Mt. Rushmore. I do not have trouble with motion sickness, but the first couple of times I almost puked. The noise of the engines was deafening. We wore special flight helmets with headsets, and it muffled some of the engine and wind noise.

We took classes to identify edible plants, how to make water potable, how to make a shelter from material found in the environment, and other survival issues. When I was a Boy Scout, our extended camp-outs, they taught us many of these same skills. They gave us field type compasses and topographical maps and taught how to use them. Upon completion of our classes, they would take us into the woods for simulated rescue and survival.

The day we left base by military bus, they had us up way before sunrise. They issued us large backpacks including first-aid supplies, one change of clothing, and minimal survival equipment and supplies. Included were pup-tent tarps, a knife, field shovel, tablets for making water potable and other survival gear. We carried no food and one canteen of water. We had two instructors and they divided into two groups. We hiked a good five miles into the woods.

The first couple of days were miserable with the mosquitoes eating us alive. However, we found by applying mud to our exposed skin, it prevented the biting. However, the buzzing remained relentless. Our first task was to build our personal shelter. With the tools we had, we dug into the side of a hill. We were to make it high enough to kneel without hitting our heads, and wide enough to recline. Out of branches, we made a roof and partial front. We used our pup tent tarps to cover the roof. Then we used twigs and leaves to create the floor. At night, it was cozy and if it rained, it kept us somewhat dry.

A hundred yards from our shelter encampment was a small spring, which emptied into a lake. The spring water was potable and cold. The lake was convenient for bathing and fishing.

Now that we had shelter and water, we needed to find some food sources. We had the lake for fish, they taught us what berries, roots, and other foliage were edible. We also learned to set traps for squirrels, rabbits or other small animals.

After two days, we left our encampment using our maps and compasses to navigate to a predetermined location and then return to our encampment. The instructors followed, but never interfered with our navigation. However, if we made a significant error to the detriment of our group, they were up our butts, letting us know what we had done wrong. To succeed, it required the group to work and cooperate as a team. Each day, the assignment got more difficult, with more obstacles to overcome to make it back by 2200 hours.

Our pass/fail assignment was to simulate a rescue operation requiring us to transport an injured person from handmade litter to a predetermined site where we would meet a rescue helicopter. They divided us into groups of three and we would rotate daily with one of us being the patient. Besides carrying the patient, we had to carry our heavy backpacks. We could bring one full canteen of water, but no C rations. Otherwise, we were to keep our patient and ourselves alive. The designated rescue site would take us at least three days to reach. They gave us until sundown on the fifth day to make it to our destination.

The afternoon before, we hiked several miles separating the individual groups to segregate us and create uniqueness in our individual missions. They required each group to navigate a rushing stream and rocky elevations. The foliage was in some areas thick and difficult to navigate. Although our group encountered none, there was the risk of encountering wolves and bears.

I am sure if an instructor had been with our group, he would have had a good laugh or failed us on the spot. It was the second day out and I was the patient. We came upon the stream located down a steep embankment on both sides. The lead person decided one man would stay with the patient and the other would scout downstream looking for an easier egress. We located the enhanced route, but, it required us to backtrack at least a mile through the rough terrain.

Both men carrying the litter were exhausted by the time we arrived at our area to cross the stream. As the patient, I thought it would be great fun to annoy the other two by moaning and complaining. While they took a break, I increased my complaints and demanded food and water. I was successful in being annoying and it went unappreciated.

The area of crossing required traversing several large and slick rocks. There were several spaced far enough apart you could not just step across. It required laying the litter down, one-man jump over, on their bellies, they would stretch both directions pulling the litter and patient. I would not accuse my teammates of deliberately dumping me; however, when we were crossing the second wide spaced area and I was moaning extra loud. Suddenly, I found myself submerged in the cold water.

Perhaps we were lucky, when we searched for food, we had little difficulty finding something to eat. Although, I admit, by the second day I tired of the wild raspberries and blueberries. Eating fish without cooking was not palatable either.

Somehow, we must have made few navigational errors, because after sundown on the third day we spotted and could hear the instructors at their encampment at the designated rescue site. We kept our presence unknown and enter the next morning looking fresh and unaffected.

The last of the teams to arrive was one hour after the deadline. They lectured them due to the lateness; however, the instructors did not fail them.

The next day, thinking they would take us back to the base, they told us we would hike back to our original encampment. We separated into our two groups using our navigation skills to find the quickest and easiest route to return. We made it a game by agreeing the last group to arrive would buy the first, beer for the evening when we returned to the base.

It was the first day and near sunset, our group came across a paved road unmarked on the map. We walked it for a while and spotted a country store. There was a heavyset man at the counter and he greeted us, "Well I wondered how long it would take you guys to find the store."

We laughed and looked around for what we wanted to take with us. The beer was first on the list and then we purchased cans of soups, stews, and other prepared foods we could heat right in the can.

Checking our maps, we found that by staying on the road for several miles, we would cut a half-day off in our return time. As we continued, our walk after dark, we felt confident there was no way we would lose to the other group. The afternoon of the second day, we arrived at our previous encampment. We set up, making cooking fires to eat the last of our purchased food and drink the rest of our beer.

We were relaxing, confident we won when an instructor and several members of the other group interrupted the party. We learned the other group beat us by one hour. When we were back on base, and paying our indebtedness, we found out the other group discovered the store before we did. Although no one said anything, looking back, I cannot imagine the trainers not knowing about the store or the trainees, use of it.

Back on base, we had another two weeks of classroom studies, helicopter training, and more PT. It was a subdued graduation compared to the one at Fort Benning. Jimmy and I enjoyed being back together to share our experiences and travel back home.

* * *

Our training stalled for a few weeks. We waited and it was in October, we received orders to go to Shepard AFB in Wichita Falls, TX. We had been there for Medical Helpers School and it felt comfortable returning.

Instead of them assigning us to an open bay barracks, they assigned us to the same barracks as the Airmen and Non-Commissioned Officers (NCO) stationed at the base. Jimmy and I shared a room and spent any precious free time at the Airmen's Club. They surprised us when our instructor assigned to our class, was not a PJ. He was an experienced basic trainee instructor or TI. Class 67-4 was his first experience in handling PJ Pipeline trainees and he was unfamiliar with our routines. We baffled him the first time we fell out of the barracks, did our push-ups, and chanted "One for the Air Force, One for Pararescue, etc.".

They delegated Jimmy as class leader, and after our first day, he met with the TI and brought him up to date on our routines and the level of PT we did. We did not have access to the base pool, so we added miles to our morning and afternoon runs. Our PT time was limited, spending more on classrooms and on-the-job training (OJT). We received more than our normal stares when we double-timed in formation anywhere we went.

This school was our introduction to emergency medical care and surgical assisting. We started with more in-depth anatomy, CPR, sterile techniques, inter-venous (IV) techniques, pharmacology, and other medical areas. The intent was once we finished this and the advanced course, we could handle most medical emergencies when a physician was unavailable.

It must have been comical to watch as we practiced on each other, giving injections, starting IV's, and bandages. Most of us had more than one area of bruised arms and butt. The last two weeks, we assisted in the emergency room at the base hospital.

Before we left Sheppard after six weeks, they issued us new tailored uniforms made from the same upgrade material as officer's uniforms. Even our fatigues were tailored. With each of our schools in the Pipeline, they instilled an attitude of toughness and superiority to other Airmen. Now, when we returned, we felt we were members of the elite Special Forces. For me, it went beyond, it instilled in me a self-pride I had never experienced.

* * *

Every time I returned from a training school, Gene was happy to see me. It was the first time she expressed she understood what the hard work and dedication were about. Although I had trouble expressing my feelings for her, she was always telling me she loved me. I spent more time with her, give her extra attention, and we even spent a weekend at Corpus Christi and Padre Island.

* * *

I went to my parent home in Ft. Worth for Thanksgiving, and while there, I talked about Gene or my training experiences. My dad's response was, "I can't believe my little sissy boy will be a PJ." To my dad's disappointment, I was never much of an athlete in school. I was into music and played in the school bands. I ran track my junior and senior year of high school.

My mother's curiosity was about Gene and how serious was our relationship. It raised her suspicion when I asked to bring Gene with me for Christmas. No one knew of my plans to ask Gene to marry me. With my mother's approval for Christmas, I now needed Gene to agree to go to Ft. Worth to put my plan into action.

When I asked, it excited her to meet my parents and spend Christmas with my family. Now I needed to figure out when and where I would propose.

I decided I would share my plans with Linda, Gene's roommate, and best friend. When I told her, she said, "Oh my God — You will surprise her. She thinks you got cold feet." She said, "Ask her anywhere but in your car in front of the barracks."

It was not the most romantic place, but it was a private location. One of our favorite places to spend time together was Brackenridge Park. Sunday afternoon before we left for Ft. Worth and the Christmas holiday, we went there with the pretense of a picnic and walk through the botanical gardens.

Before I had gone to Zale's and picked up the engagement ring. They gift wrapped it in a larger box to disguise the content. Gene picked up sandwiches, and I brought beer and soft drinks. When she was not looking, I put the wrapped box in the bag with the sandwiches.

At the park, we went over to a picnic table away from any crowds. As Gene opened the sack to retrieve the food, she discovered the wrapped box. She said, "What is this?"

"Just something special I wanted to give you before we went to my parents. I want you to open it now."

She looked at me and removed the wrapping. Inside the first box was another gift-wrapped box. She laughed, "Is this a joke? How many more boxes do I have to open?" I smiled and kept quiet as I watched her open the second package. They filled the second box with tissue paper and the ring box was in the center. When she saw the ring box, she cried. "Oh my God—You little devil—what did you do?"

"Before you open it," I said, reaching over and holding her hand, "Will you marry me?"

"You little devil, you tricked me. Yes—Oh yes." The tears of joy were streaming down her face.

I took the box from her hand, opened it, and placed the ring on her finger. She grabbed a tissue from her purse and wiped the tears. She said, "I can't see it for the tears. It's the one I picked out at Zale's isn't it?" I nodded my head. "I can't believe it. It perfectly fits." She turned, put her arms around my neck. "Oh Ken, I love you and you have made me so happy. Oh yes—I will be proud to be your wife."

The next few days before we left for Ft. Worth, the word got around at both of our dental clinics; they teased and congratulated us. I picked Gene up after work on December 23 to drive to my parents. I was eager to share our engagement and show off my fiancée to my family.

The forecast for the Ft. Worth–Dallas area and south, was cold temperatures, rain, and turning to ice. Rather than stop in

Austin for dinner as planned, we picked up burgers and continued to drive hoping we could make our destination before the road got worse. We were north of Waco with still one hundred miles to go when the overpasses iced up. As we progressed further north, the roads deteriorated. It was midnight by the time we got to my parents home.

I rang the doorbell and Dad answered. "We were about to give up on you and go to bed."

"Yeah, we had bad weather most of the way up from San Antonio. We hit ice about 100 miles south of Ft. Worth. I had to drive slow." As we walked into the foyer, I introduced Gene. "Dad, I want you to meet Gene." Dad gave her a hug just as Mother walked into the foyer. "Mother, I want to introduce you to Gene."

Mother stepped forward to greet Gene with a hug. As they separated, Mother spotted the ring. "Oh my, is it what I think it is? Oh, let me see it."

Gene blushed, "Yes it is."

Mother turned to Dad, "I told you, Glenn. I bet they came up here engaged. I was right." She then turned to us, "Congratulations." Speaking to Gene, "I'm not surprised. Ken has been talking about you for the last six months. I am happy for both of you."

Christmas day was a joyous occasion introducing Gene to my family. We received our share of teasing. Everyone kept telling me how beautiful Gene was and wanted to know how I hooked such a pretty one.

Gene requested we leave a day early so we could spend time together before returning to San Antonio. We stopped in Austin and spent the day and the next spending a romantic time together. Late afternoon, we checked out of the hotel and returned to Lackland.

Chapter Five

When Gene and I returned from Ft. Worth, Jimmy had orders to leave January 2 for San Diego Naval Station and Scuba school. Three weeks later, I received mine. It was the first time we did not room and train together. It felt odd not having Jimmy with me. I had made friends with other trainees in our class, so I was not alone.

Of all the earlier training, I felt this was physically the hardest. The Navy Seals were in charge and they wanted to make sure we knew they were the toughest of all the Special Forces. As far as combat trained, the Air Force was at the bottom. At San Diego, the Seals referred to us as "The Girls". In this class, the Air Force had only six trainees and we bonded and defended ourselves from the harassment.

It was not funny at the time, but now I can laugh at it. The first day of training in the pool, instead of them issuing us wetsuits like the others, the Air Force group received women's one-piece bathing suits. We gritted our teeth, donned them, and entered the pool with whistles and catcalls. After everyone had their fun, they gave us our wetsuits and allowed to change.

It became obvious why our earlier training had emphasized swimming endurance. We returned doing five hundred meter swims daily and then they added a killer workout. We swam underwater the length of the pool (twenty-five meters), jumped out, and did two pushups. Return underwater to the other end, and we added two more pushups. We continued this until you could not go further and they hauled a few men off the bottom of the pool. To make this even more difficult, the instructors at both ends harassed you.

Besides the extreme physical demands, we did our usual five-mile runs, mornings and evenings and double-timed everywhere we went. The Navy did nothing to make our accommodations comfortable; we were back to old run down open bay barracks with no heat or air conditioning. They forced the Air Force group to wait outside if a team of Navy Seal trainees arrived at the chow hall the same time we did.

They introduced us to the scuba gear and we stayed in the pool until the instructor felt we had achieved the level of proficiency to move forward. I found two things difficult, first relaxing and breathing naturally with the regulator and second adjusting the buoyancy system. Your buoyancy system required you to calculate your weight, plus the weight of the equipment you wore. I took several dives and screw-ups before I mastered the buoyancy system.

My first saltwater dive was memorable. They dropped us into the bay one hundred meters from this huge aircraft carrier anchored and under repairs. We were to dive deep enough to swim under the carrier and then ascend to a marker one hundred meters on the other side. The only information we had to adjust our buoyancy was the ship drew between fifty to seventy meters; plus we were to stay fifteen meters below it. Again, I missed my buoyancy calculation with too much weight. I struggled with the currents as my body was drifting downward. It was such a weird experience looking up and seeing this massive ship above you.

Our training progressed with several dives like the ship dive, then to further depths to where you had to regulate your ascent for decompression. With each dive, I got more confident and relaxed and I enjoyed the dives. While the Seal's trained for munitions usage, they gave our group training on an emergency rescue for downed pilots in the ocean. It included simulating a rescue of a NASA flight capsule. We practiced jumping from a hovering helicopter as part of rescue simulations.

Our final exam for PJ trainees was two different rescues. They took us several miles out from the San Diego Bay, to an area outside of the channel markers where the currents were not as strong. A Navy Tender protected the area from ships or boats entering the dive area. They divided us into teams of two and taken out in a Naval helicopter. Part one was to rescue a down pilot with the aircraft still afloat. We hovered about fifty meters from the down aircraft. We jumped in wearing full scuba gear, swam to the aircraft, and retrieved the strapped in dummy. Assuming the pilot was unconscious, we swam another two hundred meters alternating carrying the dummy with your teammate to a Navy training boat. With five-foot seas, the hardest part was getting up on the aircraft to retrieve the dummy.

The second part of the exercise was to rescue a distressed diver and bring the body to the surface. My partner and I went to the designated maker by the training boat, along with a trainer who would analyze the exercise. We entered the water and dove to seventy meters. We found a dummy entangled in a parachute and its cording. While my partner cut and de-tangle the parachute, I simulated resuscitation by using chest compressions from behind and sharing my oxygen. Once we had the victim free, we began our slow ascent simulating sharing our air with the dummy. When we surfaced, our training boat had moved two hundred meters and we again swam to the boat trading off carrying the dummy.

We returned not knowing whether we passed or failed. Failure meant you they set you back two weeks in the training and you repeated the final exercise. The next morning after returning from our five-mile run, they posted our results. My partner and I had passed. In the afternoon, we dressed in our Class-A uniforms and attended graduation. They pinned us with a silver emblem resembling a diver's helmet. In the Air Force, we did not always wear our scuba emblem; however, when we did we placed it an inch above our jump wings.

We celebrated at the NCO club after six-weeks of strenuous training. The Navy Seal trainees again harassed us; however, it did not matter since we finished and they still had several more weeks of training.

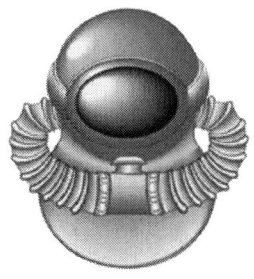

* * *

When I returned, Jimmy brought Gene and met me to the airport. We did not make it back to the base; we stopped at our favorite bar off base. I woke up the next morning in my bunk in the barracks not knowing how I got there. When I met Gene for dinner at the hospital mess hall, she was angry with me. When she shared what Jimmy and I had done the night before, I could not blame her. She accepted my apology and then switched to teasing me.

* * *

Gene started her campaign to set a date for our wedding. I continued to avoid discussing with her, my inevitable deployment to Vietnam. I was skeptical setting a date not knowing when my training would complete and how afterward I would ship out to Vietnam.

Again, I went over to talk with Sergeant Kelley for his advice. From what I knew, and he confirmed, I had two schools yet to attend before PJ graduation. I did not know it but while I was at Fairchild AFB, he had dental work done and Gene had assisted the dentist. When he found out she was dating me and later she became my fiancée, he promised to pull strings and find out when I would leave for my next school. Sergeant Kelley felt confident if I put in for leave time to get married, they would adjust my last school to after the honeymoon.

With this information, Gene and I set our wedding for May. Gene had the full burden of planning the wedding. I would not be around to help. Her mother could not help and when she found out the wedding was at a base chapel and not a Catholic church, she declined to come. Unbeknownst, Gene accepted my parents' help with the reception.

Gene's roommate was her maiden-of-honor and worked to help Gene with all the preparation. I asked Jimmy; to be my best man and he did not hesitate to accept. They promoted Gene to E-3 or Airman Second Class, and the extra money helped. Personal credit in 1968 was scarce, but both Gene and I had joined the Credit Union at Lackland. They loaned us enough to pay the wedding cost.

* * *

The first week of March 1968, Jimmy and I left to meet with our class at Gunter AFB, Montgomery, Alabama. This was the first time the entire group of Class 67-4 had been back together since Fairchild AFB.

When we began, they told us this would be a pass or fail school, and failing meant they would drop you from the program. We lost classmates with scuba school, but only because they dropped out, not because they failed. With Survival and Scuba, if you did not pass, they set you back and repeated much of the school. The tension escalated when they said they could drop us. Class 67-4 was down to ten.

Along with our normal vigorous PT, we started with intense classroom courses on anatomy, pharmacy, and emergency medical procedures. The pace was fast and the testing tough. There was no more going to the club for beers in the evening and social activities on weekends. Every night and weekend, found us in the barracks studying. We broke into small groups with leaders who excelled in a subject as tutors. It was cram for a test and start over for the next one. I contribute it to our teamwork during this period we lost no classmates.

After four weeks of non-stop class work, they took us out into the field for another application of emergency treatment simulation. Since our class was small, now ten, we set up an encampment in the Alabama woods and worked on the project as one team.

The simulation was a down troop carrier aircraft with variations of injured and dead. To make this more realistic, they brought students from other schools at Gunter, created realistic looking injuries, and held the exercise at night. They had brought in a fuselage of a transport aircraft, lit fires in strategic areas, and scattered debris and the patience. It was so realistic looking; you were caught up in the emotional urgency and seriousness of the exercise. We set up triage and then we treated the injured, most crucial first and then getting the survivors ready for helicopter transport. Our instructors observed and recorded every little detail.

The next morning, we listened to the instructors' detailed assessment. Afterwards, we would don our heavy backpacks for a ten plus mile hike in the woods. While gone, the training team set up another simulation for the evening's exercise. We did this for three days before returning to Gunter.

They gave us the weekend to recuperate, and then they assigned us to Gunter's emergency room for OJT. After six weeks, there was no graduation ceremony. We returned to our assigned bases more mentally exhausted than physically.

This time when I returned to Lackland, they assigned Jimmy and me to Wilford Hall Hospital's emergency room and surgical services. They put us on the rotational schedule, working day, and night shifts. This great experience would become invaluable later.

* * *

When I returned from Gunter AFB, Gene was completing the last details of our wedding in May. Every available time I had, she had me involved in some manner. Gene and my mother were having a conflict over serving alcohol at the reception. I initiated a truce and compromise. A champagne toast would be the only alcohol satisfied my mother's Baptist beliefs.

Gene and I found a one-bedroom furnished apartment a few miles from the base. I moved in, Gene stayed in her barracks until after we married. We set the wedding for Saturday afternoon on May 18, 1968. When my parents came down from Ft. Worth, they took over our apartment, and I stayed in the barracks with Jimmy.

Gene's father had died when she was a teenager, her mother refused to come to San Antonio; she asked the dentist and his wife she had worked for the last two years to stand in for her parents. They had a young daughter and she was our flower girl. The wedding was to be small, with a guest list of less than fifty. Most were friends we worked with at Lackland. While Gene had no family in attendance, my parents, my older sister, an Aunt and two cousins with their spouses attended.

The day seemed to come quicker than Gene and I expected; however, she had worked hard and had everything organized. As I stood up front of the chapel watching and waiting for the procession, Jimmy poked me, "What's going on Johnson? You are as white as a sheet. You okay?"

He snapped me out of whatever mystical trance I was in and I said, "Yea, a piece of cake." The music swelled, I watched as Gene came down the aisle, and I realized I was in love with her. Perhaps I had ignored my feelings. It had been an intense year and I had spent it apart from her. The emotions as I watched her come towards me and stand next to me were deeper than I had ever experienced. I smiled at her and then turned my attention to the chaplain.

I heard the chaplain's words and I repeated the vows, however, I was again in a fog. Again, Jimmy snapped me out of it when he handed me the wedding ring. When I placed the ring on Gene's finger and looked into her eyes, it confirmed God had blessed me with a beautiful and loving wife.

The reception went well, although, the photographer irritated me by interrupting for more pictures. Jimmy's toast was comical and embarrassing at our naivety while dating. He said you could set your watch by observing my car drive up in front of Gene's barracks every night. Everyone knew the relationship was getting hotter, by watching the car windows steam up.

Gene and I took two weeks of leave time for our honeymoon if you want to call it a honeymoon. To satisfy her mother, Gene agreed we would drive up to her Mother's home so she could meet me. We drove up to Austin our wedding night and stayed there for a day. Then, we took a two-day drive to Kankakee, an industrial and farming community about sixty miles south of Chicago.

Meeting Gene's mother (Mary) for the first time, I understood why Gene never wanted to visit her mother. Mary was domineering, abrasive, and self-centered. Although she treated me graciously, watching the way she spoke to Gene and her younger siblings was embarrassing and I felt sorry for them.

While there, Mary was relentless in insisting we get married by a Catholic Priest. It did not matter to me and when Gene gave in to her mother, we had a private ceremony at Mary's church.

We took a detour rather than driving directly home. We spent five leisurely days returning to San Antonio. It still gave us several days of bliss, time to set up our apartment and send out the thank-you notes for the wedding gifts.

Gene went through the process using the Lackland's legal offices to change to her married name. Gene had always stated her parents had expected and her dad wanted a boy. They had picked out Gene as a name and when she was born, they never changed the spelling. Gene said she always hated having to explain why her name was in the masculine form. She surprised me when along with her married name; she changed her first name to Genie. The name change seemed to fit her and it was easy to transition.

Chapter Six

It was in June, Jimmy and I received our orders to report to Eglin AFB, Florida for Survival Evasion, Resistance, and Escape (SERE) School and Helicopter Flight School. At Eglin was the 48th Aerospace Rescue and Recovery Squadron and we would complete our training there.

When I requested the extra time for my wedding, they moved me back to Class 67-5. Jimmy wanted to graduate with me; he requested and postponed his last schooling. He never told me until the day of the wedding. For me, it confirmed he felt the same as I did about our friendship.

Eglin was an old base near Fort Walton Beach on the northwest coast of Florida. The facilities along with its age were in disrepair in our training area. However, the main base and its supporting facilities were up-to-date. The flight line (runways) was extensive, and the Air Force could land any aircraft they had. A refurbishment and routine maintenance squadron were at Eglin and the maintenance of the Eastern Air Force's fleet was there. It was a busy hub for the Air Force.

PJ training facilities were in an old abandoned area. Except for those assigned to the training squadron, most of the base did not know of the facilities. I believe they wanted it that way. We were back to them housing us in old World War II vintage open-bay barracks with no mess hall accommodation. They trucked meals out to us, or if we were in the field, we ate C-rations.

We felt as if we were back at Lackland during our pre-Pipeline days. They required us to do the pushup and pull-up routine entering and exiting the barracks. Our NCOIC was a veteran PJ from the Korean War, Master Sergeant O'Connor. He was unrelenting with his physical expectations and stamina of his trainees. He also expected nothing less of his training instructors.

Sergeant O'Connor could not have been over five foot six inches and one hundred fifty pounds. Although he was twice the age of us, he kept up or exceeded us. It was embarrassing when I was dragging my butt after an intensive exercise and I would look at Sergeant O'Connor and he was barely sweating. You even heard the instructors moan when Sergeant O'Connor would push us harder.

It was after two days of nothing but PT training, and we were in formation after a five-mile run, Sergeant O'Connor addressed us. "At this point in the training, we are not here to drop anyone from the program. If you made it this far, you have what it takes to be a PJ. What we want to instill in you, is the mental and physical toughness required to survive the rescue missions we will call upon you to execute. After leaving your training, it's imperative you maintain this level of physical conditioning. We know there are always casualties in any war; it is our responsibilities to ensure you are not among them due to our failure to prepare you. And now," he paused for emphasis, "if you get a big head and think you have made it; think again. I promise I will ride your rag-bag assess until you drop before I let one of you leave my training without being qualified to wear the uniform of a PJ." Again, he paused, "Do you understand me?"

We had heard similar speeches before, yet coming from this veteran and with such emotion, for me it hit home. We answered in unison, "Yes Sergeant." I was obsessed, brainwashed, fanatical, 'gung-ho', or whatever you want to call it. I was soon to be a PJ and could not believe I had actually done it.

Every day we remained at Eglin, I pushed myself more. Jimmy teased, "What the hell happened to you, Johnson. Someone lit a match to your ass?"

Week three we joined an Air Force Officers group (Second Lieutenants) who were undergoing flight training. They too were here for SERE school. They joined us for a week of PT training, but they didn't expect them to keep up with our rigorous routine.

Week four they separated us into groups of four or five and instructed us there would be no segregation or acknowledgment of rank. We were here for the same training if we found ourselves behind enemy lines.

With only a small backpack containing minimal survival gear, we hiked out into the woods and a swamp area south of the base. The area was a designated reserve area. Jimmy and I teased, "Reserved for what? Nothing, but alligators, rats, and snakes would live here." Reading the issued topographical map was essential in survival. Miscalculations would find yourself lost and life threatened.

The first night, we scattered into the woods to survive, moved or hid to evade them capturing us by our simulated enemy. I do not remember why, but they named me team leader. If captured, the team leader was to assume the role of the officer in charge (OIC).

It was within four hours of leaving our encampment my group heard voices. We could not tell if it was another trainee group or the enemy. I decided we should hide in the adjacent bushes until we could distinguish who they were. As we hid, the voices got louder and we determined they were the simulated enemy by the comical Asian accent they were using. Although we stayed hidden, it was as if they knew where we were.

They closed in; one man was standing within feet of my location and directing the others to spread out. I held my breath thinking I could keep hid when I felt a boot kicking my leg. The voice said, "You come out, now." I did not move. "Come out now—I shoot." I was kicked again and then felt the barrel of a rifle in my ear. "Come out—Raise hands—I shoot." He jabbed me in the ear with the rifle.

I stood up, raised my arms above my head, and looked at a man I had never seen before, in fatigues, no rank insignia, and his face darkened with camouflaged paint. There were at least eight others and within minutes, they had captured our entire group. The only thing that I could conclude, they were hiding in the area before our arrival and watched us.

They tied our hands behind our backs and blindfolded us. With them blindfolding us, it eradicated any attempt to determine the direction and distance we were being taken. Although they injured none of us, they were rough moving us along to their encampment. Anytime you resisted, they shoved or punched you. At their encampment, they separated and placed us in separate small rooms barely large enough to fit. You could sit upright, but could not stand or lie prone. I could see around my blindfold, but I was still in complete darkness and the walls of my cell were concrete, but the floor was dirt.

Although I knew this, was a simulation, with the total darkness, the lack of voices or other sounds, the effect was realistic and I found myself apprehensive. Time seemed to crawl and I had no idea how long they held me in the cell. They took me to what I assumed was an interrogation room. With each question, I replied with the taught response of name, rank, and serial number.

They taunted, threatened, pushed, and punched me; however, I gave no answers to their inquiry.

This time they placed me still blindfolded and tied, into a room I could stand and move about. I sensed it before I realized there were other men in the room with me. By whispering, I determined only one other man was there from my group and they had captured and interrogated everyone. They never removed me from the room. When they removed most of the others and then replaced them with other captives.

It was hours later, they untied us and they removed the blindfolds. We were in a concrete-walled room with dirt floors. The ceiling was twelve feet and up next to the ceiling was two small windows allowing for ventilation. From the windows, we realized it was after dark. We had lost any perception of time. There was a bucket over in one corner, which served as our latrine. Even getting near it, the stench was nauseating. We perceived they had captured us for twenty-four hours and none of us had anything to eat or drink. Without sleep and nourishment, our stamina was getting low.

After they left us alone for a couple of hours, my group whispered about what to do. I said, "Hey guys, this is a SERE course. We flunked the evasion part, how about us trying to escape?" The door was secure and anytime the guards came, there were at least three. Overpowering them would not work. Someone suggested we attempt to go out the window. We hoisted the smallest man upon the shoulder of our largest man. By pulling himself up, he assessed the situation. He said there was nothing between our building and the woods behind it. He also saw no evidence of lights or guards. We agreed, even if they caught us escaping, sitting here waiting for the next round of interrogation was not acceptable. Attempting escape had to be the next obvious progression in the class.

We kept listening for any activity and when we heard nothing, we started our plan. We would hoist each other to the window. By hanging from the windowsill, we would pull the next in line until everyone was out. Once on the ground, we would run to the edge of the woods and keep watch for the next escapee. Once the whole group assembled, we moved away from our captive location.

The reality we had actually escaped without detection seemed unrealistic. We sneaked away and were two hundred yards away when suddenly several spotlights hit us. Dejected, we stopped and raised our hands in surrender. Rather than met by our previous enemy, Sergeant O'Connor and several other instructors met us.

Sergeant O'Connor announced, "The game is over. You have completed the exercise."

We waited with another group who had preceded us in their escape until all the captured groups had escaped or remained captured. No group had eluded capture; so, it verified our enemy knew of our location from the beginning.

They critiqued our performance; we learned the exercise lasted over two days. This further emphasized the important training we received. Back at the barracks, with a hot shower and a meal, they gave us the weekend to relax and celebrate. Eglin had a great NCO club they allowed us to use and use it we did.

With our SERE school completed, we were back to our daily intensive PT, interlaced with classroom lectures reviewing, and testing on previous school material. Twenty members of Class 67-5 joined 15 of Class 67-3. There was class rivalry and Sergeant O'Connor and his staff encouraged it. Even our five-mile runs became competitive. We continued for two weeks until we started flight training.

* * *

This was our first introduction to the three types of rescue helicopters we would train and eventual use. The first was the Bell UH-1 "Huey" and the Army use it as troop carriers, gunships, and medical evacuation (Medevac). The Air Force ordered modified versions of the Huey (UH-1H) and PJ's used it in Vietnam. Transport capacity was three litters on racks and one on the floor. A few Hueys had an external hoist system, but most required the PJ to repel using ropes. The Huey had two seven mm machine guns mounted at each side door. The Huey flew with a crew of four, pilot, co-pilot/navigator, flight engineer/gunner, and PJ who doubled as an added gunner when required.

The next was the HH-43 "Huskie" or as Pararescue named it "Pedro". It was tiny compared to its contrasting CH-3 "Sea King" and later HH-3E "Jolly Green Giant". The design of the Pedro wasn't for combat due to its slow speed and short range. Although, the Air Force modified it with external fuel tanks, and Pararescue teams used it in Viet Nam. Transport capacity was two litters on racks and one on the floor. A disadvantage of using the Pedro was they didn't build it with armament. The Pedro flew with a crew of four, pilot, co-pilot/navigator, flight engineer, and PJ. Its rescue hoist system mounted on the top and outside the aircraft.

The main aircraft in the arsenal of the Air Force Pararescue was the Sikorsky HH-3E or Jolly Green Giant. Most Air Force models were for Combat Search and Rescue (CSAR) due to the required long-range operations, hovering qualities, and in-air refueling capabilities. In designing the Jolly Green, they built extra armament and protection in to protect its crew. It had two seven mm machine guns on each side doors and a third at the rear cargo door. It flew with a crew of five, pilot, co-pilot/navigator, flight engineer/gunner, and two PJs.

With its rear cargo ramp access and large cargo area, its capacity was twenty-five passengers or fifteen littered patients. Although its capacity was valuable in medevac operations, we rarely used it for medevac. We kept it in reserve for the critical emergency rescue missions over Laos, Cambodia, and North and South Vietnam. The rescue hoist system mounted right above the right door used to deploy the PJ and recovery of the rescued patient easier. Both side doors had extra steel protection as did the body of the aircraft. Specialized pontoons could attach to the side of the aircraft for water rescue missions. Along with its sophisticated communication systems, the Jolly Green Giant was invaluable to air operations in Vietnam and was the resulting component that saved lives rather than lost or captured.

* * *

Previous training with helicopters at Fairchild AFB had been with the Huey. Any practice deployment we repelled using ropes to drop while the aircraft hovered. When we first started aircraft training again at Elgin AFB, we again used the Huey. Our first simulation of retrieving a patient using a litter and hoist system, they brought in a Pedro. Elgin only had two Pedro. One we could use for training, and the other remained for emergencies on the flight line. If we were lucky, they trained us using it.

When we trained using a hoist system for deployment and retrieval, we used the "horse collar". It got its name because it looked like an oversize horse collar. Where it attached to the cable was a six-inch round devise named "the donut". PJs named the cable ' the idiot cord'. In Vietnam, PJs would hook their rescued patient in the horse collar and ride up standing on the donut and holding on to the cable. Hence, the name 'idiot cord' for the individual's reckless way of using the hoist retrieval system. We would have received more than our butts kicked if we even attempted doing it in training.

When we practiced using more complex rescue exercises, they brought in the larger CH-3 or "King" for short. Along with the flight crew, there were four trainees and an instructor. We thought the Huey was noisy, the roar of the turbo engines made communication other than radio headsets or hand signals impossible. We began our exercises in cleared areas using the horse collar and basket litters. Then we advanced to wooded areas and the distance to repel and retrieve was greater.

Eglin had several HH-3E or "Jolly Green". However, they assigned them to the flight training school. When we advanced to practicing water rescues in the Gulf of Mexico, they sent two Jolly Greens with pontoons attached. During our training, we observed flight trainees doing exercises where they used the pontoons to land on the water. Although, none of our exercises did the Jolly Green ever land on the water.

It was my second water rescue and I was aboard a Jolly Green. I assumed the exercise would be like the first one where they had a simulated jet crash in the Gulf. We jumped into the water, swam over to the aircraft, pulled the dummy from the cockpit, swam away from the aircraft. The helicopter hovered above us and they sent the cable down. Then we strapped the dummy and ourselves into the horse collar and they retrieved us.

This day, we flew further away from the coast and when the aircraft descended, we saw a NASA Gemini spacecraft bobbing in the Gulf with a Navy Tender securing the area. Our aircraft hovered about two hundred meters away from the spacecraft and lowered to less than twenty ft. Three trainees including myself jumped into the water, swam over to the capsule. There were no dummies or individual to rescue, but we were to board the floatation collar and open the hatch. We then swam away from the capsule and they retrieved us using the horse collar.

Although NASA commissioned the Air Force using trained PJs, this was the closest to a NASA rescue mission all but a few PJs ever got. Due to our utilization in Vietnam, the Navy took over as the primary rescue team during the NASA Apollo missions. Back at Lackland, Jimmy and I bragged and embellished to our friends we had trained with NASA.

Most of the three-plus weeks when we were training with helicopters, because of the number of trainees, and the limited aircraft, you spent much of the time waiting your turn. However, the instructors did not allow us to just sit around waiting. We were out running through the woods or practicing emergency medical procedures on each other.

When we returned to our barracks after our flight training, Sergeant O'Connor insisted on three more grueling days of PT. We even ran seven miles to the Gulf, swam to a marker at least two hundred meters and back. He gave us a short break before we returned to our training area. That day, Sergeant O'Connor accompanied us and duplicated everything we did.

* * *

The day before we graduated, we packed our duffle bags and moved to a vacant barracks the flight training school used. The next morning, we did not vary from our routine; we completed our five-mile run. After breakfast, we showered, dressed in our Class A uniform, and double-timed in formation over to the parade grounds. Sergeant O'Connor led our formation along with all the PJ instructors. It was a special day for Class 67-5 and our sister class 67-3. Along with our graduation ceremony, there was a class of flight trainees (pilots) getting their wings. All units along with a band marched in front of a reviewing stand.

As we passed the reviewing stand, I noticed a Colonel wearing a burgundy beret. Up to then, I did not even know there were PJ officers. This Colonel was the CO of all training squadrons and he was here to present our Pararescue Flash (emblem). In the military, rank has its privileges (RHIP), we waited until the officers from the flight training school finished their ceremony; we then began ours.

They call our names alphabetically; we each moved forward, came to attention, and saluted the Colonel. Next to the Colonel assisting were Sergeant O'Connor and another instructor. Sergeant O'Connor removed our garrison cap, and the Colonel replaced it with the burgundy beret with the Pararescue Flash attached. He then pinned our flight wings above our jump wings. We saluted again and returned to our formation.

U.S. Air Force Pararescue Flash

With the ceremony completed, the band led us again in formation pass the reviewing stand and off the parade grounds. Once our two classes hit the street, we stopped, broke out in a rehearsed "Ooh-Rah—We Do These Things, That Others May Live". We then double-timed back to our barracks singing our cadences.

U.S. Air Force Flight Crew Wings

Waiting for our return, were a barbeque and a beer wagon set up behind our barracks. There were lots of backslapping and hugs. When I hugged Jimmy and stepped back, we both were fighting tears. I knew then, not only had I made a buddy for my military career, I had made a friend for life. The party continued into the night.

Jimmy and I fighting hangovers grabbed an early morning military bus to the airport. In Dallas, even with our military standby preference, they bumped us from our connecting flight. There was not another flight to San Antonio until 6 PM. We headed for a bar.

During our wait, it hit me. I was now a member of the military's Special Forces. I had accomplished everything it took to elevate myself to those standards. It confused me to how I really felt. I think it takes someone who has been in the military's Special Forces to understand the self-pride and the commitment it takes to serve your country, especially during a war. You know you will put yourself in harm's way, however, your dedication pushes it aside, and you do not think of the danger.

Looking back, although, they told us our training was just as intense and detailed as previous trainees, it was not. Meeting and working with veteran PJs, they trained and prepared them more for the arduous duties we faced in Southeast Asia. Reading about the current Air Force's PJs, their training and rescue missions, makes my experiences trivial. However, I do not want to imply the PJs I proudly trained and served with were any less brave or sacrificed less. We, like those who served before us and those who followed, gave our heart and sometimes our lives to ensure we left no man behind and to save as many lives as possible.

Pararescue Creed

It is my duty as a Pararescueman to save life and to aid the injured. I will be prepared at all times to perform my assigned duties quickly and efficiently, placing these duties before personal desires and comforts. These things we (I) do, that others may live.

Chapter Seven

In September 1968, after graduation and returning to Lackland, the waiting game began. Even when I asked, no one could answer how long I would wait to receive my orders for Vietnam. I gave Genie extra attention knowing our next separation would be for a year.

Genie sensed my feeling; she said nothing; but, she made our time together enjoyable and romantic. I felt especially protective and returned her affection.

Six weeks after we returned from Eglin AFB, they notified Jimmy and me they promoted us to Buck Sergeant or E-5. I had only been in the Air Force two years and most Airmen were lucky to make this rank by the time they ended their four-year enlistment. We credited our promotions, to completing Pararescue Training.

About the same time, Dad retired from the Air Force after over thirty-three years of active service. Genie and I went to Ft. Worth and attended his retirement ceremony both dressed in our military uniforms. The base press and later the <u>Air Force Times</u> published an article and pictures of Dad, Genie and I in their publications. They introduced us to the Base Commander and General conducting the service and the press picked up the uniqueness of our family. The article focused on the father with thirty-three years of exceptional service, a daughter-in-law likewise in the Air Force and the son wearing the wings and beret of Pararescue. I watched Dad beam with pride.

* * *

Back at Lackland, they assigned me to the surgical section assisting surgeons, cleaning the surgery suite, sterilizing the equipment and instruments. After standing assisting for a long procedure, I asked myself, what happened. I spent a year training to get away from assisting dentist and here I am assisting again. Although it often got monotonous, there were those procedures, which were intense, life saving, or enlightening.

Not every day in a surgical suite is always serious and repetitive as portrayed on TV and movies. Many surgeons can be and often are clowns to break up the gravity of the procedures. They often tease with the anesthesiologist or surgical staff once the patient is asleep. Just as most professions, comical instances happen.

I scrubbed for what was supposed to be a quick and routine procedure. Once we started, no one was in the room except the surgeon, the anesthesiologist, and me. We were doing a circumcision on an adult, and this was my first of this type procedure. There were manuals for setting up the variety of procedures, telling us the required instruments, etc. I looked but did not find the procedure listed. I went to the head surgical RN for help. She instructed me to use the same setup as any skin procedure such as a cyst, and mole removal.

I followed her instructions and we began the procedure. The patient was asleep and the surgeon had started when the patient got an erection. I handed the surgeon extra gauze to handle the increased bleeding. Without even looking at me, the surgeon yelled, "Capsule."

"Excuse me," I replied.

"Capsule—Airman—Give me an ammonia capsule"

I got flustered, knowing I did not have one on the tray. "Sorry Sir, I don't have one."

The patient's erection continued and the bleeding increased. "Damn it—Get me a fucking ammonia capsule—NOW."

The more flustered I got, the more the surgeon angered, and the anesthesiologist got hysterically laughing. Finally, the anesthesiologist got up, went to a cabinet, found an ammonia capsule taped to the inside cabinet door, popped it under the patient's nose and the patient's erection subsided. However, his laughter continued and was contagious until the surgeon joined him at my expense.

* * *

In late October, Jimmy met Genie and me for lunch in the mess hall. "I've been trying to get a hold of you for days. Can I join you for lunch?"

Genie spoke up, "Of course you can. How have you been?"

"I'm doing okay." Looking at his face, I knew he was nervous. "I got my orders for Vietnam. I am to report to Travis in two weeks. I'm going home for a week first and then to Travis from Houston."

"What base are you assigned?" I said.

I looked over at Genie, and she had this look of gloom. She knew if he were going now, I would not be far behind.

Jimmy said, "It's Pleiku."

All these months in training, they told us where we might be deployed us. There were detachments at most of the larger bases, but I had never heard of Pleiku. "Where is it?"

Jimmy said, "I checked and Pleiku is over inland from Da Nang. I understand the Army and Air Force jointly run the hospital. The Army has two squadrons of helicopters and the Air Force has a squadron of fighter jets and support operations. It's not a big base, but has lots of action."

"How did you find out so much?"

"I called Sergeant O'Connor. He told me there were five PJs due for rotation out of the 38th ARRS. I'm the first in our class to go."

Genie spoke up, "You have to come over to the house for dinner before you leave?"

"I'll make time, just tell me when." Jimmy came Friday night and Genie outdid herself with a great dinner. However, Jimmy and I drank before dinner and continued for the rest of the night. Jimmy was too drunk to drive and he spent the night on our couch.

Jimmy left the following week for home and then on to Vietnam. I wondered if I would see him once I got over there. Genie gave him our mailing address and made him promise to write. However, it never happened.

* * *

After Jimmy left, my apprehension was all-consuming waiting for my orders. I had heard some Airmen were exempt from going to Vietnam because of being married. While in the Pipeline, they told us PJs were not afforded that privilege; we were too indispensable.

So why was there a delay? Ever since Jimmy left, Genie's cheerfulness when we were alone had turned to gloom. She valiantly tried to hide it and I attempted to ignore it. The waiting game was killing us.

November 15, I got a call from Base Personnel to report. I expected this daily and felt prepared. I was wrong. I had orders to report to Travis AFB on December 10, 1968, for briefing and eventual deployment to Pleiku, South Vietnam.

The reality hit me as a ton of bricks. Now I felt nothing but insecurity and some fear. I worried how I would tell Genie and how she might react. With all the negative thoughts running through my head, I forgot the positive. I was station the same place as Jimmy. Now I knew how Jimmy was feeling when he left.

I dreaded the thought of breaking the news to Genie. I had not talked with Sergeant McInnis since Dad retired. Somehow, I knew he would support me and I was not disappointed.

He said, "You wanted this and you trained hard. You should be proud of yourself. Be careful; remember your training and you will come home safely. And yes, ask your dad to keep me informed how you are doing."

I next called Dad, "Hi, I'm glad I got to talk to you instead of going through Mother."

"What do you mean?" he voice sounded as if was irritated.

"I need some advice and you have been through this more than once. In addition, you're my dad and I know you'll be honest with me."

"What is all this mystery? What the hell is going on?"

"I got my orders for Vietnam today."

"So? You knew it was coming. It shouldn't be a surprise"

"I don't know how to tell Genie. How did you always tell Mother when you got orders separating you two?"

"First thing, don't hide it from her. Women have an intuition when something is going on. Hold nothing back even if you know it will hurt her. It's all about trust; believe me, I know. It is a given she will be upset and nothing you can say or do will prevent it. So stand strong and give her as much support as you can."

There was a pause in the conversation, and then he said, "You know you will get hazardous duty pay while you are over there. You will not need much money in 'Nam'. I would recommend keeping a few dollars for yourself and sending the rest back to the credit union. Base Personnel will help you with it."

"That's a great idea."

"You know we will keep in touch with Genie while you're gone and we will drive to San Antonio to visit. You need to focus on your job and do whatever is necessary to come home safely."

"Thanks Dad for the advice. You'll tell Mother for me, won't you? I'm hoping we can come up for a weekend before I have to leave"

"When and where do you have to report," he asked.

"Travis on December 10th."

"You know your mother will want to have a family gathering before you leave. You will hurt her if you do not make time. How about Thanksgiving?"

"I don't think there will be a problem with me getting the time off. They told me at personnel I could have up to two weeks before I leave. It will depend on Genie and if she can get the time off."

"You let us know when you are coming and then let your mother do whatever makes her happy. Okay"

Dad and I talked a few more minutes with him giving me the same speech I got from Sergeant McInnis. When they stationed Dad in Korea, he flew in and out of Vietnam. He knew firsthand the dangers of being in a combat zone. He said, "Don't be stupid. Think about your wife and family before you take an unnecessary risk. It's all about doing your job the right way and not getting your butt shot. Understand?"

Instinctively, I answered, "Yes, Sir."

When I returned to the hospital, they told me I was needed in surgery for a burn patient who had just come in Medevac. I scrubbed and joined the surgery team of two doctors, a nurse, and two medics. The surgery took longer than anticipated and it was sometime around 6:30 when we finished. I came downstairs to the mess hall. Genie and I often met there when one of us worked late. When I got there, I spotted her sitting with some friends. I said, "Have you had dinner?"

She smiled at me and answered, "No, I was waiting for you."

I leaned over and gave her a quick kiss, "How about we go to the barbecue place on 410?"

"It is okay with me. Anything is better than this chow hall food these days."

While driving, I rehearsed in my mind what to tell her and I hoped I would choose the right words. When we arrived at the restaurant, I ordered a wine for Genie and a beer for myself. When our drinks arrived, I took a deep breath and looked at Genie. "I've got something to tell you." I watched as her smile disappeared and replaced with anxiety. "I got my orders today for Vietnam." Genie's eyes turned red and the tears started, but she did not say a word. "We knew this day was coming soon. Now the waiting is over."

She grabbed a tissue from her purse, wiped her eyes. "When do you have to leave?"

"I have to be in California, by December 10th."

"That's not even a month," she said raising her voice. "Do you know where?"

"Yeah, the same place Jimmy went, Pleiku. Please don't get upset with me. Please believe me when I tell you how difficult it's for me."

"I don't think so. I think you want to go over there." I had never seen her with such a hateful look. It reminded me of the hateful looks her mother would give her.

I said, "You're wrong and you know it." I reached across the table to hold her hand. However, she pulled away. "You know I love you and I don't want to leave you." I paused attempting to find the right words. "The reality is I am going to Vietnam and I will be back in a year. We have talked about this, and we made our plans. "

"It was your plan. I never agreed to any of it." Her reaction and raised voice confused and angered me.

The tears caused her makeup to run down her cheeks. She grabbed two more tissues and wiped her face. "I'm sorry. I thought I was prepared for this day. I'm not. Why did you bring me here to tell me? I'm so embarrassed. People are looking at us."

"I don't know why I brought you here. I thought it would be easier." Her look had softened, yet her eyes filled with tears. "I was wrong. I'm sorry."

"Can we eat and go home?"

I agreed and we finished our drinks before they served our dinners. However, when our food arrived, neither one of us had an appetite. Genie said, "Can we go home?"

I agreed, paid our bill, and we left. There was silence on the drive home.

When we arrived, Genie went into the bedroom pulled her uniform off, threw herself across the bed, and sobbed. I followed her and tried to comfort her. She looked up at me and pleaded, "Please, just leave me alone. I need some time alone. Please — Just leave and close the bedroom door."

I changed into my blue jeans and I grabbed a jacket and closed the bedroom door. I went over, grabbed two beers from the refrigerator, and walked out of the apartment. I started walking aimlessly. I was choking back the tears and I was hoping I could find a quiet secluded spot to sit and think. I was feeling so guilty I had hurt Genie. I found an old tree across the street from the apartment complex and I sat down against it drinking my beer.

After about an hour, I looked up and I saw someone walking across the parking lot. It was dark and I did not recognize the person at first. As the person got closer, I realized it was Genie. She walked up to where I was sitting, and said, "Are you okay?"

I got up, opened my arms and she melted into them. "Yeah, I think so, how about you?"

"I will get through this somehow. However, one thing I will promise you, I won't be okay until the day you return. Do you understand?"

"Yeah, I do. You don't have to say anything more. I understand. Please try to believe me when I tell you I am sorry for hurting you."

"I'm scared for you. It's the stupid war which worries me most." I held her tight and kissed her tenderly. She had no more tears in her eyes, "Let's go home. I want you to hold me until I fall asleep."

Genie agreed to go to my parents for Thanksgiving. We went up on Wednesday evening after work. Mother had invited all the family who lived in the Ft. Worth area. The house filled with family for Thanksgiving. The atmosphere was festive, although, there was an unspoken somber feeling.

The next day, I took Genie shopping at the mall. I wanted her to pick out something for Christmas since I would be absent. We walked the mall twice with her unable to decide. In frustration, I pulled her into a jewelry store and bought her a small gold heart on a fine chain.

While in the store, I put it on her and made her promise, "I want you to wear this while I'm gone."

She smiled at me, "It will never come off."

We returned to work on Monday and the days flew. I reserved the final week to spend alone with Genie. We spent our time in a daze not wanting to be apart and we rarely answered the phone. We went out to dinner each night and we spent extended mornings in bed. She tried her best to be in good spirits; however, I could see the stress and the red eyes from crying.

Chapter Eight

On December 9, 1968, Paul and Kathy our friends, drove Genie and me to the airport. They issued me a military standby ticket to San Francisco with a layover in Denver. I was dressed in my Class A Blues with my wings, beret, and polished jump boots. I carried myself with pride and I wanted everyone, especially other military, to recognize me as Special Forces.

Time came for me to board and Genie would not turn loose of me. Paul had to pull her from me so I could board. As I boarded, I was fighting the tears. Once we were in the air, a flight attendant asked, "Are you heading for Vietnam?"

"Yes, Ma'am."

"Our pilot said if you are, the drinks are on us. So what will you have?"

The layover in Denver was longer than expected. My original flight was full and it was two hours before I could catch the next one. There was a military check-in station at the San Francisco airport and they told me there was a bus to Travis in an hour. I grabbed my duffel bag and found a bar while I waited.

On the bus, an Army sergeant checked my papers against his roster. We drove out to Travis AFB where they dropped us off at the temporary barracks and showed us the mess hall. They told me someone would contact me in the morning and take me to my security briefing.

The next morning after breakfast, I went to an office complex and entered the door marked, 'Security Briefing - Authorized Personnel Only'. There were four Green Berets and two Army Rangers waiting. In a few minutes, two Air Force Captains (pilots) joined the group. Our duffel bags where piled up against the wall.

One of the Army Rangers looked as if he recognized me. "Weren't you at Ft. Benning last July for jump school?"

"Yeah I was," pointing to my jump wings."

Across the hall was a conference room. A Colonel from the Air Force, two Majors, and a Captain who were Army Rangers waited for us. They began by reminding us of our responsibilities to the United States if captured by the enemy (e.g. name, rank, and serial number only). Then they continued to discuss the status of the war, and where intelligence reported the Viet Cong were assembling or moving. They spent hours describing intelligence and covert missions conducted all over Southeast Asia. Once the meeting concluded, they reminded us the information we received was top-secret. I walked out wondering why I needed briefing. What difference did it make where the enemy was?

I carried my duffel bag into the barracks and caught the Army Ranger I had spoken with earlier. We walked together the few blocks back to the NCO Club where we had dinner and a few beers.

* * *

They had us up before 0400 hours, and after we had breakfast, we went to the flight line. One hundred plus men from all branches of the military boarded a commercial jet. Within the hour, we were airborne. We flew first to Anchorage, Alaska and then on to Yakota, Japan. When we left Yakota, our flight attendants were not with us. Our destination was now Tan Son Nhut AFB, near Saigon. The closer we got to our destination the apprehension was stifling. Those who had been vocal were now silent while those like me got giddy and talkative.

Our arrival was very much the way they portrayed it in the movie *Platoon* when Charlie Sheen arrives in Vietnam. The only difference was it was a cold and rainy late afternoon. It was total bedlam with at least twenty aircraft of all sorts and sizes parked in no particular order. Military vehicles of various types were running around carrying men, fuel, and cargo to and from the aircraft. It was haunting to see among the cargo, those black bags which contained the bodies of valiant men who given their lives.

Once off the aircraft, we went to a large metal hanger where we waited in lines to check on our transportation to our final destination. A group of twenty men, mostly Army, were going to Da Nang. They directed us to a C-130, parked two hundred yards from the hanger. By the time, we walked carrying our duffle bags and loaded, we were soaked.

They loaded the aircraft with supplies and there was barely enough room for us to sit in the wall mounted jump seats. Once everyone had boarded, someone from the cockpit yelled, "Everyone sit down. We're taking off." The engines roared and the whole aircraft shuddered as we accelerated down the runway. Our flight was an hour and the landing was anything gentle.

Again, we waked over to a metal hanger and stood in line to be check against the roster. The Army corporal who checked me in, looked at me, "Who in the fuck are you? You must be some special motherfucker. They sent a Huey for you. Go over there where the Major is standing." I walked over to the Major, saluted him, and then introduced myself. He told me he was Dr. Santos. I could tell by the way he looked at me that his curiosity about my burgundy beret. "You going to Pleiku," I asked.

"Yea, I am." He continued to look at my beret and then at my jump wings. "Why are you wearing the beret?"

I straightened up, squared my shoulders, and I pointed to my flash. "I'm Pararescue."

He still looked confused, "Pararescue, what's that?"

I apologized, but I had to laugh at his ignorance. "I'm Special Forces; a PJ. I am trained for search and rescue."

He shrugged and tried to break the formality. "Where are you coming from? I was doing a residency in Surgery at Wilford Hall at Lackland AFB."

"I'll be damned. I was at Wilford Hall too."

An Army Warrant Officer interrupted our conversation. He asked, "Are you Major Santos and Sergeant Johnson?"

"Yes Sir," I answered.

"OK, grab your gear and follow me." We walked across the tarmac to a Huey like the Bell helicopter I had trained in the previous summer.

Once on board, I heard the pilot check with the tower and then shout, "Hold on." The engines roared and he lifted straight up with the nose pointing down at a forty-five degree angle. I looked at the Major who was white around the mouth and his face beet red.

I yelled, "First time on a Huey, Doc?" He nodded, then leaned over, and puked. The pilot increased his speed; altitude, banked left, and the doctor puked a second time.

We got wet from the rain, with the doors open, and when the wind shifted. After less than an hour flight, there was more radio chatter; I could see an airbase as we descended. The pilot banked the Huey hard to the left brought the nose up and landed without a bump.

Major Santos looked at me, "Do you really fly in one of these?"

"Yes Sir."

"God, I hope I don't have to ride in one of these things again." With his fatigues and boots covered in puke, I could not help myself and laughed. He gave me an annoyed look and then he too laughed.

* * *

An old World War II vintage jeep ambulance was our transportation. An Army corporal dropped the major at the hospital and me at my barracks. Instead of the customary barracks, these barracks were rows of metal and concrete Quonset huts. They placed them into the ground with only the roofs and a few feet of walls exposed. Windows were next to the roof to allow some light and ventilation into the rooms. The door was three or four steps down. The floors were concrete; there was a long center hallway with doors off both sides and lit with a series of bare bulbs. Half way were the showers and latrine. Compared to the outside of the buildings the inside was clean and odor free.

I had my duffel bag on my shoulder and I was looking for someone to tell me where my room might be. I found a man coming out of the shower. "Hi, I just got here, I'm Sergeant Johnson. Do you know which room they have me in?"

"Fuck if I know. There are three empty rooms, take any one you like."

Not only was I confused, I was exhausted, "Don't you have roommate assignments?"

He gave me a look as if I was stupid and then realized I was new. "Hell no, we have private rooms in this barracks."

I learned later that this was an NCO barracks. I selected the room at the end of the hall, thinking it would be quieter and it had two windows. The room was small, maybe eight by ten feet with a single bed against the outside wall, a desk next to it with a dresser and open closet on the opposite side.

There was a light knock at my door and when I answered it, there stood a young Vietnamese boy with a pillow, blanket, sheets, and towels in his arms. "Me house boy. Welcome. Me fix you bed, okay?"

Looking down at him and feeling surprised I replied, "Sure, thank you."

"You take shower? Me fix you bed." It sounded like a great idea since I had not showered in two days. I opened my duffel bag, pulled out my shave kit, and headed for the showers.

It surprised me when I returned to my room. The houseboy had my bed made and was unpacking my duffel bag. "I come tomorrow, iron clothes, okay?"

"Ah, sure." I pulled a dollar from my billfold and handed it to him."

"No — No. Me no take American dalla. Only MPC. Pay me tomorrow, okay?"

* * *

The next morning, I dressed in clean fatigues; I grabbed my raincoat when I heard the rain on the roof. Before leaving, I saw a man in the latrine. I introduced myself and then ask directions for the mess hall.

After breakfast, I inquired the location of the hospital personnel office. The Private told me, "It's in Building D next to the hospital." He gave me directions and as I was making my way, a jeep ambulance came by. The driver rolled down the window, "If you're heading for the hospital, I'll give you a lift."

I ran over and jumped in. "Thanks, I just got in last night."

We introduced ourselves and the corporal said, "I've got three months, two weeks and a wake up." I gave him a puzzled look and he explained, "Once you been here six months, you start your countdown."

He dropped me off at the front door. My orders stated they assigned me to the 38th ARRS, Detachment 9, (Pleiku) and backup to Detachment 7 (Da Nang). I was to report to Pleiku AFB; base hospital. After signing my paperwork, the airman gave me direction to surgical section of the hospital. I thought, shit, do not tell me I will assist in surgery. How about my flight crew?

What I found as the hospital wasn't anything I expected. I assumed they would be like other small Air Force base hospitals. They were a series of buildings with wings going off in every direction. Covered walkways connected most buildings. As with most buildings I had seen around the perimeter piles of sand bags.

I found the hospital's administration offices and checked in with Technical Sergeant Williams. Sergeant Williams was a large black man about six foot-three inches and two hundred fifty pounds. He looked like a lineman for the Dallas Cowboys. He was soft spoken, but he spoke with a southern accent. "Sergeant Johnson, when did y'all get in?"

"Last night."

He spotted my beret in my hands, You the PJ replacement."

"Yes Sir."

When he completed the paperwork, he explained they didn't wear my fatigues in Viet Nam. I had noticed the uniforms everyone was wearing looked different, but gave it no more thought. "I'm sending y'all over to Base Supply and they'll issue new uniforms. Tell them y'all on a flight crew. Flight crews have different ones. Y'all need new boots too."

"Yes Sir. Am I assigned to a specific flight crew or what?"

"Yeah, I'll find out which one. Come see me in the morning and we'll find them.

"Yes Sir. What time do you want me here?"

"Ah shit son, y'all going to be working your ass off. Don't worry about the time. Be here sometime before noon. Go to the NCO Club tonight and enjoy it while y'all can."

He gave me directions to the Base Supply Depot and the NCO Club. I headed out the front entrance; I noticed the same private who drove me over was leaning against a post smoking. I smiled at him and gave a nod.

"Hey Sarge, where you headed?" he inquired.

"I need to go to the Base Supply Depot."

"No use you walking. I'll take you."

I got in and he explained they used these old ambulances for transportation around the base and carrying the wounded. He said, "There's nothing going on. I'd rather drive than sit on my ass."

He dropped me off and I found the Clothing Supply section. They had two Airmen and a Staff Sergeant working at desks, but there were at least six female Vietnamese working at sewing machines. When I showed my papers, the sergeant said, "Go over there and see Mama-son. She'll take care of everything for you."

I was there over three hours, and when I left, I had four pairs of fatigues and four flight suits, all tailored. I had three pairs of boots and was different from any I had seen. The toe and heels were leather, but the rest was a green canvas.

The new fatigues were similar to my old fatigues, except they were a darker green with black camouflage patterns; the blue nametags and stripes were now black. The jump wings above my left chest pocket were also in black. My flight suits were a lighter material and were one piece, which zipped and buttoned up the front. There were more pockets strategically placed on the arms, and legs. These were the same flight suits I was so familiar growing up as an Air Force dependent. Because we were in a war zone, flight suits had no rank insignia.

As I left, I asked for directions to my barracks. This time I had no ride, so I had to hoof it for two miles. On my way, I passed the Base Exchange (BX). The BX exchanged my US currency for MPC.

When I got to the barracks, several of the doors were open, and music playing. I stopped and introduced myself. One guy when he noticed my beret, said, "Oh shit. We got another one of those crazy rescue boys living with us."

I smiled and asked, "What do you mean?"

"Oh nothing, we had one of them, um, you call yourselves PJs; right? You guys got to be fucking crazy to do what you do."

I just laughed it off. "I suppose we are." I learned why people thought of us in this way.

Walking into my room, I noticed he had made my bed as we did in basic training and the floors swept and mopped. I looked over at my closet and my uniforms were laundered, starched, ironed, and arranged.

I heard a soft knock at my door. I opened it to find the same Vietnamese young man; he walked right in and asked, "You like?"

I responded, "I am very pleased. I just can't believe you did all this."

His smiled, and he looked at my new duffel bag on the floor. "What inside?"

"My new uniforms." Pointing to my old ones, "I can't wear those." I could tell he didn't understand. I pulled a new set from the bag.

"Oh—Yes—Me fix new clothes?"

"Okay" I pulled out my wallet and handed two MPC to him. He smiled and explained in his broken English that for three MPC a week he maintained my room and do my laundry. This was great, I didn't have to make my bed or clean my room. If I put my dirty clothes in the laundry bag, he returned them clean and ironed. I handed him four MPC, he shook his head and handed one back. I explained, "No, please keep the extra MPC. I need the new uniforms washed and ironed today. Okay?"

He smiled, took the money, and grabbed the duffel bag. "Me go fix clothes. Okay"

I found out they had named this young Vietnamese man Tommy and was twenty-three, but he looked sixteen. Later, I found out the going rate was two MPC per week and Tommy had gouged me, but I did not care. Tommy had my room looking perfect and my uniforms were always flawless.

Chapter Nine

Remembering what Sergeant Williams had said, I decided I would check out the NCO Club. It was only 1600 hours, a little early for dinner, but I had not had lunch, so I left and went to the mess hall for dinner. They told me the mess hall was open 24 hours and you could get breakfast or dinner at any hour.

The NCO Club was very nice inside. A beautiful bar of mahogany ran almost the full length of the building. There were tables set into rows around a small dance floor. Vietnamese males and females were working and they dressed in white shirts, black slacks, and black bow ties. Like most clubs, the lights were dim and each table had a small oil lantern adding to the ambiance.

A waiter escorted me to an empty stool at the bar. The club was not busy, yet there was around 30 Army and Air Force enlisted men drinking and talking. I ordered a beer, sat back reviewing my first day in Viet Nam. I knew it would not be like this all the time, but how bad could it be? It would not take long for me to find out.

I had been sitting there an hour when I noticed three Airmen coming in and one was wearing a burgundy beret. I thought I had better go introduce myself. Then I recognized the person; it was Jimmy.

I got up and rushed towards him, "Jimmy. Hey Jimmy!"

He looked my way and a big smile erupted on his face. "OH MY GOD! Is it really you Johnson?" We first shook hands, looked at each other, and then hugged. "I can't believe you're here. When did you get here?"

"Last night, sometime. I haven't gotten use to the time change."

"Don't worry about it. There is no day or night here. We work around the clock." He introduced me to the other two men. Both of them worked in surgery and we would be friends. "God, I can't believe you got stationed here. This is really great."

Finding Jimmy was euphoric and I relaxed. Although he was giddy and talked my ear off, his eyes told me another story. He looked stressed and tired. I sat the rest of the evening with Jimmy and his friends each one telling me what it was like here. If I was to take them at their word, it did not sound good. Nevertheless, beer and war stories always lead to exaggeration. Jimmy told me his barracks were two down from mine. He had just finished a mission towards Cambodia and then followed up with six hours of surgery.

He said, "I'm off the schedule for 24 hours, but it don't mean shit. If we can, let's meet here again tomorrow night."

* * *

The following morning I headed back to the hospital around ten. I checked in with Sergeant Williams. As soon as he saw me, he said, "Your crew is waiting on y'all."

"Great. I'm eager to meet them too." I followed him out a rear door and we headed over to the flight line in a jeep ambulance. We went to an area of the flight line, which must have had at least 30 Huey's lined up in these cubicles off to the side. The roar of engines warming up was deafening. I saw at least 10 of the aircraft with Red Cross emblems; the rest appeared to be armored gunships. Just as the one, I rode coming from Tan Son Nhut, they all had guns mounted on both sides.

With all the aircraft, and many with crews working, somehow Sergeant Williams found mine and said, "Da Nang told me until y'all were assigned to a Detachment 9 team, y'all work with these guys." The introductions went around. Warrant Officer (W-2) William Curtis, or Billy, was the pilot and CO. Warrant Officer (W-1) Lawrence Lipinski or Larry was our navigator and co-pilot. He was second in command. Corporal Julio González and Sammy White were the flight engineers and gun operators.

They all seemed friendly. Except for Julio, all had only been here a short time. When Julio greeted me, he said, "I got 5 months, 21 days, and a wake-up." Although Billy, our pilot, had only been here a few days, this was his second tour. He was a veteran of this war.

The whole time we were talking, we had to yell due to the numerous Huey's starting up their engines and then lifting off. It seemed as if when one left, another returned. Billy came over with a flight helmet, "Let's get this adjusted." I could tell by looking at the helmet it was not new; it had scuffmarks all over. I looked around for Sergeant Williams, but he had left.

Once Billy had the helmet adjusted, he said, "Come on board and let me get you acquainted with our bird. We need to get airborne in a few minutes. There is nothing like breaking in a new guy by getting his feet wet."

"We have a mission already?" I asked, almost frightened by the prospect.

"It's not a rescue mission, if it's what you were asking. We will help out with some Medevac in an area about 50 klick from here."

I followed him on board and he first familiarized me with the communication systems. He then showed me some safety gear in case we went down. He showed me four wall lockers, two on either side of the opening in the wall separating the cockpit area from the rear cargo area. The two upper lockers on each side contained my equipment and medical supplies. The other two were storage for emergency equipment and small arms ammunition. On the back wall were more lockers for ammunition for the two side guns. In the center were racks for three litters, one above the other. In the opening between the cockpit and the rear area, was my jump seat, which folded up against the wall. There were jump seats against the back wall, although, the two gunners rode standing up with a safety harness attached to the gun mounts.

Billy opened one of my lockers and said, "I don't know what all of this stuff is, but the back pack is worn anytime we are in flight. It contains communication equipment for when you leave the aircraft and the rest is medical shit. You probably know what it is." I took a quick inventory of the backpack, the supplies, and equipment in the lockers. We had trained at Eglin with the same gear. As I was busy with this, I heard Billy asking Julio, "Are we fueled and ready?"

Julio replied, "Yes Sir. Fueled, system checked and fully armed. We are ready on your command." Julio had a big grin on his face enjoying his sarcasm. Billy acknowledged him with a middle finger salute.

Billy raised his voice, "All right guys, let's load'em up, and get this bird in the air." As he passed me into the cockpit, he pointed to a pistol in my locker, which was in a leather holster. "Doc, get your gear on and it includes the pistol." I gave him an affirmative nod as he and Larry sat in their respective places and strapped in.

I no more got my pack back and holster on, adjusting the straps and belts, when the engines started up with a roar. As soon as I plugged my helmet into the radio system, I could hear Billy and

Larry going over a checklist. Then Billy said, "Doc, sit down and strap in. I don't want to lose you on your first flight." I pulled the jump seat down and strapped myself in. I looked up and we were already lifting off. Billy got twenty feet in the air and then he kicked the engines in the butt and banked the aircraft to the left and up. There was all this chatter between Billy, Larry, and the tower. The tower was not commonplace; it was a bunker building out between the flight line and the runways.

Once airborne, we joined three other Medevac copters and headed toward our destination. With the roar of the engines and all the chatter on the radio systems, it was hard to concentrate let alone understand what was going on. Even with my mike an inch from my mouth, I yelled for them to hear me. At one point when the radio chatter was quiet, I asked Larry what to expect. He said, "This is nothing more than a regular Medevac. We volunteered so Billy and you could get your feet wet. As we reach the area, they give us our landing coordinates, we'll pick up anywhere from three to five wounded and then get the hell out of there. We'll return to base and then do the same thing all over again."

"I thought you said Billy's been here before?"

"Yeah, this is Billy's second deployment, but it's been over a year since he was here. After a few times, he will be one hundred percent. As for you, you are green. Pay attention and remember we work as a team."

"Where do we put five stretchers in here?"

"We put three on the racks and then lay the other two on the floor. It's tight, but it works."

"How in the hell am I supposed to take care of these guys? There won't be any room to work."

Billy spoke up, "You're not supposed to. The medics on the ground get the injured ready for transport. We swoop in, load'em, and then get back as fast as we can. Unless there is an emergency, you should not have to do anything. Hell, most of these Medevac units do not even have a medic onboard. We are the exception. With you on our team, we will not do this all the time. We will do search and rescue too."

"Okay," I said. "I think I understand."

The radio chatter picked up and Billy told us, "Heads up guys, five minutes to target. Recon says them bad boys are still in the area." We maintained our formation with the other three copters and made a wide sweep of the area as we lowered our altitude. When Billy made a right turn, I could see the ground from my position in the aircraft. What I saw I was not expecting. I do not know what I thought it would be, but this was not it. It looked like utter bedlam. There were people running around like crazy; smoke was everywhere with rifle and heavier artillery fire was going off. Contributing to the chaos not too far off were fighter jets dropping bombs and rockets. I said to myself, we are going down there?

The thought no more crossed my mind when Billy made a hard bank to the left, then down. I looked over my shoulder and could see red and blue smoke marking our landing area. I heard Billy in my ear. "One minute to touch down, everybody be alert." Within thirty seconds, Billy had us on the ground. He lowered the engines, but did not turn them off.

I unbuckled and started for the door. Sammy grabbed my arm, "Hold it Doc. Let'em bring'em to us. Julio and I will handle getting'em in the racks. Your job is to check'em out real fast, make sure they lie still and then get back into your seat. We will be in the air in less than five minutes."

By this time the men on the ground where running at us with the wounded. My stomach turned when I saw head, chest, and leg wounds. As each stretcher arrived, Julio and Sammy worked in synchrony as they reached over, grabbed the bars, lifted, and swiftly placed each of the injured in the racks. A fourth injured they placed on the floor parallel to the others on the rack. I checked vitals of each man and assured them we would have them to the hospital in no time. All gave their acknowledgement except for one. The fourth man had a head and a chest wound. His vitals' were not critical, yet it he seemed disorientated and glassy eyed. I learned the drug of choice given before transporting was morphine. They determined the dosage based upon how vocal and combative the patient.

Upon securing the fourth man on board, I heard Larry yell, "Doc, buckle up. We're in the air in one minute." The engine roared again and I buckled. We lifted a little slower; maybe it was the additional weight or all the activity close to our bird. Once we ascended fifteen to twenty feet, Billy once again kicked it in the ass, banked away from the action and gained altitude.

Radio chatter slowed down when we got to our cruising altitude. I unbuckled and went over to the man whom I thought was going into shock. His vitals were slipping; he was turning ashen and I got no reaction from his eyes when I yelled at him. I went to my locker and grabbed an IV kit and a fluid bag. This man was already in shock and I thought that maybe some quick fluids might stabilize him. I got everything set up; as I was about ready to go for a vein, our bird made a drop and then banked back up. I yelled, "Hold it steady for a minute Billy. I'm trying to get a fucking IV started."

Billy yelled back, "What the fuck are you doing up. Get your ass back up here!"

"This guy will not make it if I don't push fluids in him "

I heard Billy reply, "Oh, Shit!"

I got lucky and hit the vein with my first attempt, I taped the needle in place, and then hand pumped the fluids in as fast as I could. When I checked his pulse, it was a little stronger. His eyes were still non-responsive and his color continued to deteriorate. I grabbed a second bag, I hooked this one to the ceiling, and let gravity do the work, however, opened the stopcock wide open. I headed back to my seat and buckled in.

As we approach the base, I saw at least eight or ten ambulances awaiting our arrival. Upon landing, Billy killed the engine and an ambulance backed up next to our bird. The blades were still turning with less than two feet of clearance above the vehicle. Julio, Sammy, and I helped unload each patient and watched the ambulance head for the hospital.

I took my helmet off and found some clean gauze to wipe my face. I was sweating like crazy even with weather over cast and in the sixties. I noticed Sammy standing off to the side smoking. I walked over to him and bummed one. I had not smoked in over a year and it made my head swirl. I had all these wild thoughts racing through my mind and I was just trying to get myself to calm down. Sammy was teasing me about my first time.

Billy walked over and said, "I need to talk to you." He turned to Sammy, "If you will excuse us Sammy."

"Yes Sir," Sammy responded. "We gonna go out again?"

"Yes just as soon as we can get refueled. Can you supervise it?"

Sammy walked off and Billy turned towards me. "I don't want us to get off on the wrong foot. I am in charge of this team and I dislike giving orders. I prefer instead to ask you and I expect you to follow my request. I asked you to get back to your seat and you ignored me."

I interrupted Billy pleading, "Sir, the patient was in shock and had lost a lot of blood. If I didn't get some fluids in him, he would not have made it by the time we got back."

Billy paused and his stern look softened, "You are probably right. For medical stuff, you are in charge and the crew and I will do whatever you need. Just so you know, if I would have had to make an evasive move to avoid incoming fire, you could have fallen out. You are a valuable member of this team and I will not risk your death to save some grunt who may or may not make it. If you have a patient who needs treatment to make it back, if I can without putting us in jeopardy, I will give you the time. Once I give the command we are lifting off, you are to buckle in and you stay there. Are we clear on this?"

I could feel my face flush, "Yes Sir. I understand."

"Look Doc, I don't like this rank shit and you do what I say or else bullshit. This is my second tour. When we work as a team and look out for each other, then we all get to go home upright and not in a box."

I did not say a word, but I knew I had screwed up and Billy was right. I also realized I had a lot to learn in a short time to be part of the team. Within twenty minutes, they had us refueled, and we were again airborne with three other units. My first day, we completed three more Medevac transfers; however, on the last trip we only brought back the dead.

* * *

When we landed after our last trip, it was getting dark and I caught a ride to the hospital. I went to check with Sergeant Williams, but he had left for the day. The posted duty roster did not have my name, so I left heading back towards my barracks and stopping off at the mess hall.

After a long shower, I headed to the NCO Club to meet Jimmy. By the time I got there, Jimmy was already shit faced. I needed to talk to someone about my day. When I told Jimmy, his drunken response was, "Yeah, Johnson. Look—your first days are shit. Hey, every day here is shit. You won't survive if you let it get to you. Come on, have another beer, and let it go."

I stayed long enough to have two or three beers and listened to the bullshit the group with Jimmy was spewing. I kept waking-up all night seeing the faces on some of the people we brought in and wondered if the more critically wounded made it. I kept hearing Jimmy's voice telling me to let it go. I kept asking myself, how do you do it.

* * *

I had been there over a week when they notified me to contact the CO of 38th ARRS Detachment 7 at Da Nang. I could contact him by radio from our bird. He told me Captain Atkins was my assigned flight commander. He flew a Pedro and currently assigned to Da Nang. When he returned to Pleiku, they would assigned me to him. Until then, I was to continue working with the Army flight crew. He also stated, when I could get some time, he wanted me to come to Da Nang for a briefing.

Over the next few weeks, it was almost a daily routine of Medevac missions. There was heavy fighting in the western highlands and there seemed to be a constant stream of wounded and dead. I kept thinking, why did I go through all of this training, just to ride back and forth carrying wounded? Occasionally I started an IV or re-dressed a wounded area. Otherwise, I rode and watched the price our men were paying for this war. The only way I found to combat the sleepless nights was to get shit face like everyone else and crash back in the barracks only to repeat the same horror the next day. I was just doing Medevac; I had nothing going on at the hospital.

One day we had just completed a second Medevac trip and it appeared it would be another long day. As we landed, Billy got a radio transmission. We had a classified rescue mission. There was crew waiting to refuel and check out our bird; I asked Billy, "What's going on?"

"Doc, you're going on your first rescue mission. I hope you put on clean shorts this morning," he teased. Then in a serious tone, "They won't give us our destination until we are in the air. You know all the security bullshit stuff." We were in the air within minutes and the tower instructed Billy to change radio channels. When he did, they told him we would look for a downed F-100. Two A-1 Sandy's were already in the air in route to the last known location. They also gave instructions we might have to fly under radar detection.

Billy instructed us, if we had to fly low, there was to be radio silence. "Doc, I want you helping Larry to communicate with the Sandy's or the downed F-111. He gave me the separate channel settings to listen for any radio chatter.

Within thirty minutes, one of the Sandy's had located the wreckage. He called out, "Rescue nine - five; this is Sandy three - seven. Copy?"

Larry responded, "This is Rescue nine-five; go ahead"

The Sandy gave us of the coordinates and notified us there were hostiles in the area. His radar was picking up potential SAMs (Surface to Air Missiles) in the area. The other Sandy was in route to help with clearing out any hostiles who would inhibit our rescue. He recommended going low to avoid the SAM detection system.

Billy lowered our bird barely above the trees. I swear we were so low the belly of our bird scraped some of the treetops. It was scary yet exhilarating watching the skills of Billy handling our bird. From then on, I had full confidence in his aviation skills. When we were within 10 klicks, Sandy three–seven, notified us the area was clear.

Billy circled the area and we all looked for hostile activity, but saw none. We could also see the Sandy's firing on targets a short distance from us. Billy broke radio silence and said, "Doc, I will set us down and you jump off. When you find the pilot, let me know and I will come back in for you. Got it?"

"10-4" My backpack had a small radio transmitter, plus a beacon if they lost visual contact. Billy really did not land, but hovered about six feet off the ground. I jumped and headed for the aircraft. I hooked my helmet to the radio in my backpack. Before I could reach the aircraft, I heard Larry's voice yelling, target at 9 o'clock. I turned to my left and I saw the pilot waving at me from some heavy bushes. I turned toward him and ran to his location. We moved back under the canopy of the brush. "You okay?"

It was an Air Force Captain and there was blood trickling down the side of his face and more blood staining the left upper arm of his flight suit. "Yeah, I think so. I bumped my head a little and I twisted my left ankle. Boy I'm glad to see you guys, it was getting a little scary around here."

"Okay Captain, sit down over here and let me take a quick look at you and then we'll get the hell out of here." I cleaned up the cut on his forehead and it would need some stitches. I checked the shoulder and it was just a minor cut. I cleaned and bandaged both. I next checked the ankle and it did not appear broken. I took off his boot, wrapped it, and put the boot back on. "Captain, let's see if you can stand on the ankle." He did, but it was too painful to put his full weight on it.

I was about to call in for our recovery when I heard Larry's voice. "PJ nine - five; we are drawing some fire. Can you be ready in five?"

"Rescue nine - five; we're ready now."

"10-4. Stay undercover until you see us coming in."

"10-4"

I turned to the Captain, "Our bird is on its way in. We'll stay here until we see them make their approach. Then, we will make a run for it. I want you to put your left arm over my shoulder and take as much weight off the ankle. It will hurt, but we have to move fast. We got some bad guys coming our way." The Captain acknowledged me.

Within minutes, I had a visual. Billy made a quick circle checking the area before making his quick decent. As soon as I saw the decent, the Captain and I started for the landing area. Billy put the bird all the way down but never slowed the engines. Julio helped me get the Captain on board and strapped him in a rear jump seat. Before I could get to my seat, Billy was lifting off and yelling at me to get strapped in.

We had no more lifted off when we saw incoming fire at the location the captain and I had just vacated. Julio and Sammy turned their guns and returned fire as Billy kicked our bird in the butt and gained altitude.

Larry radioed, "Sandy three - seven; this is Rescue nine - five. We have a recovery. Copy?"

"Rescue Nine - five; roger. We got your backside."

"Sandy three - seven; Thanks for the help. We owe you."

Larry contacted Pleiku tower, notified them we had a successful recovery, and gave them our estimated ETA. He requested an ambulance for the Captain. We took longer because the base was launching several fighter jets. We had not declared an emergency. We had to deviate from our return route and wait for landing clearance.

Once we were on the ground and the Captain was on his way to the hospital, I spoke up, "Okay, that was fun." I was doing my typical nervous giggle.

Both Billy and Larry told me they do not always go this smooth. I would experience the good and the bad recoveries later. Billy pulled me aside out of hearing range from the rest of the crew. "Julio and Sammy do not have security clearance. Just so, you know, we were actually in Cambodia. If asked, we never left South Viet Nam. Understand?"

"Yes Sir."

"What's this "Yes Sir" bull shit? Didn't we have a talk?" I laughed at him and gave him a cocky salute. I then returned to our bird to store my equipment and resupply my backpack.

Since we were not going out again, I caught a ride to the hospital and found them treating he captain in the ER. "I'm glad to see there weren't any serious injuries. Good luck to you Captain. I hope we don't have to meet this way again."

He smiled, "Thank you Sergeant. I agree; I don't want to meet again under the same circumstances. When I get out of here, I would like to buy you a beer. What do you say?"

"Thanks Captain, but it's unnecessary. I did what the Air Force trained me to do."

Chapter Ten

When I arrived in December 1968, I was the third PJ assigned to Pleiku. All three teams were to be flying HH-43's or Pedro's. The third PJ was a Staff Sergeant David Thompson, a second tour veteran. David arrived a few weeks before Jimmy. My tour started with me the only PJ flying with the Army. When I arrived, Captain Atkins was supporting Detachment 7 of the 38th ARRS out of Da Nang and Sergeant Berri was the PJ on board. Sergeant Berri was schedule to return stateside by the end of the year.

* * *

It was late December, when needed, I was still flying with Billy. However, Jimmy and I had begun rotating through surgery. David due to his seniority they didn't require him to work at the hospital. Every day, you did not know where you would work. Rescue and Medevac always took priority over hospital duty. I was at the bottom of the call list for rescue because my team was still flying out of Da Nang. It wasn't unusual to work fourteen plus hour shifts at the hospital, followed by a rescue mission. The pace was brutal and you lost track of time of day, day of the week, and even day of the month.

It was a Sunday afternoon; I was working triage or the emergency room. Jimmy was assisting in surgery. He finished came by my area the time my shift ended. We walked over to the NCO Club, and we were just enjoying our first beer, when an Army Corporal notified us to report to the flight line. Moaning, we left and the corporal drove us.

Expecting to either fly a rescue mission or Medevac, it surprised us we went to a Pedro we did not recognize. There was an Air Force Captain, First Lieutenant, and Airman waiting. The Captain introduced himself, "I'm Captain Atkins, and that is Lieutenant Riley and Airman Burkowitz. The Old Man, Colonel Price, said he requested you two to come to Da Nang for a briefing. Since you never showed, he sent me to retrieve you."

I said, "Captain, I talked with Colonel Price two weeks ago. He said when we had spare time to come to Da Nang. I don't know about Sergeant Douglas, but I have not had a day off since I arrived."

The Captain interrupted me, "I know Sergeant. I am here and my orders are to bring you over now."

Jimmy asked, "Do we need to notify someone, we are leaving? What if—"

The Captain interrupted again, "Don't worry about it. I have notified your CO at the hospital." He looked at me, "Sergeant Johnson, I believe they assigned you to my crew if I ever get to return to Pleiku. I inherited Sergeant Berri, but when he leaves, you might have to come to Da Nang. Anyhow, as soon as they have my bird refueled, we're leaving for Da Nang."

We loaded and Burkowitz handed us spare flight helmets. We sat in the extra jump seats and plugged our helmets into the communication system. There was the normal chatter with the tower as we lifted. I had not ridden in a Pedro since Eglin and I forgot how quieter they were than the Huey.

When we flew into Da Nang, the size of the base was relative to Tan Son Nhut. Along with Phantoms (F-4), there were Super Sabre (F-100) and Thunderchiefs (F-105) and several other aircraft I did not recognize. What grabbed my attention as we landed was the HH-3 Jolly Green's lined up in their cubicles. I wanted to see the equipment they carried. I saw another copter, which looked like the HH-3 but larger. When I asked, they said they were the new HH-53 or Super Jolly Greens.

We drove over to Detachment 7's command center. We entered a conference room and introduced to at least twenty officers and enlisted men assigned to Detachment 7. Among them was Sergeant Dean, an instructor we had at Gunter, It was great seeing a familiar face and even greater when he remembered Jimmy and me.

While the conversation was lively, several of the PJ veterans questioned Jimmy and I about our missions and our use for Medevac. All of a sudden, the door swung open and Colonel Price stomped in with his aide yelling, "Attention."

Everyone jumped to their feet, turned toward the Colonel, and came to attention. As the Colonel proceeded to the end of the table where there was a speaker's podium, he said, "At ease— Please be seated." There was rumbling and squeaking of chairs as we sat. The Colonel began, "I'm having this briefing, to bring everyone onboard to what we can expect in the coming months." He looked over at Jimmy and me, "Glad you men could find the time to join us."

I felt myself turn red with embarrassment; but, in my defense, the Colonel never gave me an order or instructions when we were to come meet with him.

The Colonel's briefing continued; we could expect an escalation in the war. Bombing and attack missions would increase to interrupt the supply routes and push the Viet Cong back across the DMZ. In doing so, we could expect more rescue missions. He said he had requested to his superiors increased number of rescue aircraft, crews, and trained PJs. The Colonel's concern was the plan called for more carpet-bombing in areas along the DMZ and the borders with Thailand and Cambodia.

Again the Colonel looked at Jimmy and me, "I have asked your commander at Pleiku to reduce the hours you are being used for Medevac in order you can be available assisting other detachments. We are ending the practice of rescue zones and we will move our resources to those areas and detachments requiring the most assistance. I would recommend you pack toiletries and a change of clothes in your aircraft. It's likely you will spend time away from your home base."

After he completed his briefing, he opened the meeting for questions. The majority of the questions were coming from the pilots. Their concerns were about aircraft maintenance and the lack of personnel at Da Nang available to keep their aircraft at the alert level. The Colonel acknowledged the problem and promised to do his best to rectify it.

The Colonel gave his aide a signal and again the aide yelled, "Attention."

Everyone jumped to their feet and watched as the Colonel stomped out. Captain Atkins came over to Jimmy and me, "It's too late to make a return flight. I'll find a bunk for you tonight and someone will get you back tomorrow morning."

Sergeant Dean was standing nearby and heard the captain, "How about I buy the first round over at the club. I'm not on the roster tonight and I hear they have steaks on the menu."

Jimmy said, "You got my attention."

Da Nang had on-base bus service. The base was so spread out the transportation was often a problem. Pleiku was small enough we could use hospital ambulances for transportation, or just hoof it. We caught a bus over to the club and spent the evening with Sergeant Dean talking about our training and what might have helped us prepare for Vietnam. He took us back to his barracks and we slept in vacant bunks.

* * *

We were up early, had breakfast and at the flight line by 0700. Captain Atkins was nowhere to be found. We ended up catching a lift on a C-130, which was making a supply run. We were back at Pleiku by noon and checked the duty roster. Neither of us were on the list, so we headed back to our barracks for a shower. We planned to meet at the mess hall around 1700 and then to the club.

I was relaxing under the shower when I heard someone call my name. Instinctively I knew what was coming and I wanted to hide. When I responded, a corporal told me I had a mission and my crew was waiting. The corporal waited while I dressed and he took me out to the flight line.

Billy had the engines running and Larry was standing out front watching for me. As soon as I got out of the vehicle, Larry yelled, "Come on Doc. Get your gear on; we needed to be in the air half hour ago."

I did not have time to get anymore than my helmet on and plugged into the communication systems and Billy was lifting. He yelled, "Doc, get strapped in. You can put your gear on in a few minutes."

I asked, "What's the scoop?"

Larry said, "We got two Huey gunships down. The Sandy says he is not sure there were survivors. There are hostiles crawling all over the area and command has scrambled support jets."

I asked, "Are we the only rescue crew?"

Billy said, "No, Pedro 4-4 left half-hour ago. He cannot get anywhere near because of artillery fire. They are sending another Sandy from Dak To.

Within twenty minutes, we contacted a Sandy. He all but escorted us over to the crash site. We were at one thousand feet and it did not look good. The wreckage spread over a quarter mile although one cabin was intact. It took another half-hour of us circling off in the distance with the Sandy's and Super Sabre clearing the area. Pedro 4-4 was flying next to us.

I heard the call, "Rescue nine - five, Sandy two - five.

Larry answered, "Rescue nine - five, go ahead."

They gave us the coordinates and Billy made the turn. We heard Sandy 2-5, tell Pedro 4-4 to maintain his pattern. Again, the Sandy escorted us in while firing in the area as we approached. Billy made a wide sweep and then as he lowered to less than two hundred feet. Sammy yelled, "We got hostile movement at 7 o'clock." Billy kicked our bird in the butt and ascended back to one thousand feet.

"Rescue nine - five, Rooster nine-err, two — two. Maintain your altitude while I make another run."

"10-4, Rooster nine — two - two; we copy."

Out of nowhere, an F-100 swooped in below us and hit the area with an onboard rocket followed by his guns. The target lit up with flames and smoke. They cleared us again for an approach. This time we saw nothing and Billy brought us in, hovered at 6 ft. and I jumped. Billy rose to one hundred feet and was making tight sweeps. I ran to the cabin, which was intact. When I got within one hundred yards, I saw body parts. The pilot strapped in was dead, but the other two-crew members were lying outside the cabin at various distances. The body parts appeared to come from one individual.

I radioed, "Rescue nine - five, PJ nine - five; copy?"

Larry responded, 10-4, PJ nine - five.

"No survivors here. Give me some direction to the other site."

"PJ nine - five, 3 o'clock and two-hundred meters."

"10-4; Rescue nine - five"

I hightailed over to the other site. I had to break through some thick brush. Once I did, I saw a burned cabin, or the remains of the cabin. I also saw severely burned bodies. I could only find what I could identify as two crewmembers.

"Rescue nine - five, PJ nine - five; Copy?"

"Copy PJ nine - five"

"No survivors here. Check on the number on board this Huey."

"10-4, PJ nine - five"

While I waited, I searched the area. The stench from the burned bodies was nauseating. I checked in all direction for about fifty meters.

"PJ nine - five, Sandy two – five, Copy?"

"10-4, Sandy two - five"

"Command says three crew on each bird. Copy?"

"10-4, Sandy two - five; thank you."

Billy called me and instructed I return to the first site. He said Pedro 4-4, was coming in to the burned site.

With the F-100 and both Sandy's, keeping watch over our backsides, Billy landed at the first site. He kept our bird running. Sammy and Julio helped me get the pilot out and put him a body bag. We gathered as many body parts as we could find and put them in a separate bag. We did not have another bag, so we used a tarp out of our emergency locker and wrapped the third crewmember. Then we loaded all three in our bird.

Pedro 4-4, landed at site two and it took its crew 30 minutes to find the third crewmember. He was not in better shape than the others were. We left before Pedro 4-4 and headed for our base. For the last month, I had hauled body bags when we did Medevac, however, this was more dismal. Perhaps it was because these were flight crews and not Army grunts. No one spoke on the return to base.

Later than evening, I met Jimmy at the NCO Club. He said, "What happen to you? I went by your barracks, and no one knew where you were." I told him of our mission and finding all the crew dead. He said, "Shit, this war is getting crazier. I still don't understand why we are trying to save this God forsaken country." I had to agree.

* * *

I had been on long day of Medevac missions. It was routine once you finished, you went to the hospital to check the duty roster for surgical assisting. I rode over with our last patient and I was taking a shortcut through triage when I ran into Dr. Santos. I had not seen him since we arrived. "Hey Doctor Santos, how are you? Where you been hiding?"

"Hey, Johnson. Shit, I was here only two days when they pulled me down to Tan Son Nhut. For a while, I thought they would make me permanent. It is one — busy — hospital. It is chaos every day. I am glad they released me. How are things with you?"

"They got me flying Medevac missions most days. I only get a rescue mission when there is no one else. I'm not even with my assigned unit. It's the shits."

Dr. Santos said, "Hey when I get off here, how about I buy you a beer?"

"Sounds great, I got to check the duty roster, then I'm heading for the mess hall. I try to catch up with you later."

As I walked away, he said, "Oh yeah, before I forget, Merry Christmas."

I had no idea it was Christmas Eve. "Merry Christmas to you, Doc." I walked to the surgical area and looked at the duty roster. Shit, I thought. They scheduled me in an hour in suite C. They penciled my name in with a question mark.

I headed for the locker room, took a quick shower, and put on scrubs. I worked straight through the night assisting with one surgery after another. All those Medevac we had hauled in during the day were processing through surgery. Any of the severe cases they flew to Ton Son Nhut or Da Nang. It was around noon when I was relieved and left the hospital. I stopped by the mess hall and enjoyed the turkey dinner they served. I returned to the barracks, pulled my clothes off and was asleep by the time my head hit the pillow. This was my first Christmas in Viet Nam.

* * *

Even though Colonel Price had told us he was pulling us from Medevac's, they never stopped. It was January and the Monsoon season had not let up. Attempting to wear rain gear while flying only made it impossible to work. So, I got soaked. By the time my day ended, I was cold and wet. I would stand in the shower to warm up.

Jimmy and I discovered an off base bar where drinks were cheap; they had Go-Go dancers and prostitutes. So many guys were going upstairs to enjoy the prostitutes; although, the same guys were at sick call being treated for their STD. You could buy Vietnamese pot and one night I let Jimmy talk me into smoking some with him. This was my first experience smoking pot, and it hooked me. It was an enjoyable high, better than alcohol, and there was no hang over. Although it was unauthorized to bring pot on base, I saw no attempt to curb the possession or use of it. Commanders looked the other way if you did not use it while on duty.

* * *

It was the week after the holidays; they notified me to report to Detachment 7, in Da Nang. The written instructions said nothing about bringing my gear. Something told me I might not be coming straight back. I went over to the flight line and they were repairing Billy's bird. I got my gear along with my toiletries and change of clothing I stored onboard. I walked over to flight logistics, found a unit, which was heading to Da Nang and hitched a ride.

When I checked in at Detachment 7 command operations, Captain Atkins was waiting. He said, "Sergeant Berri left right after Christmas. They told me I would go back to Pleiku, but it never happened. I was without a PJ; I had no choice but to use you. I hope you came prepared to stay."

Now I was glad I listened to my inner voice and at least brought my gear. "Not really, Sir. I brought my flight gear and the extra personal items the colonel told us to store on board."

Captain Atkins said he would have someone retrieve my things from the barracks if I couldn't do it myself. Lieutenant Riley took me over to the flight line to familiarize me with their bird. I rode this same Pedro a few weeks ago. On the ride over, he kept repeating this was temporary and we would soon return to Pleiku.

The set up was foreign and the communication system more sophisticated. What I had also forgotten, the opening between the cockpit and the cargo area was too small for access. There were jump seats up against the outside walls in the cargo area. Those same jump seats also doubled as your racks for two litters. It would be tight, but you could get a third on the floor, although when you did, the PJ and flight engineer had to sit on the floor. They said the cargo space for the Huey and the Pedro were equivalent. However, I always felt closed in with the Pedro.

Lieutenant Riley patiently answered all my questions and showed me all the emergency and rescue equipment. Since I had not used one since my arrival, I looked over the rescue lift system. It kept going through my mind, what happens if we get somewhere where there is ground fire. There were no machine guns. Then I remembered all the times our armed Huey would go in and the Pedro had to wait until the area cleared.

Everything operated different with Detachment 7. They had three crews, two Jolly Greens and a Pedro, which were in the alert status for twenty-four hours. Three more crews were on standby. There were sleeping quarters and a recreation area at the command center. Although when you were not on the roster, you were subject call.

They did require PJs to rotate through the hospital. Most of the PJs with Detachment 7 were veterans, and this was their second deployment in Vietnam. I always felt inferior around them, although, they were always ready to answer question or help anytime I needed it.

Our call sign was Pedro 7 - 7 and we were not on the duty roster. We were on standby the next day and on alert the succeeding. They gave me Sergeant Berri's old room in the barracks. The barracks at Da Nang were larger, but I would not say they were any nicer than we had at Pleiku. One distinction, you shared a room with another Airman. I felt fortunate my roommate was Tom Winters, a veteran PJ.

* * *

The next morning, I caught a bus over to Detachment 7 Operations. I had taken my time since no one had said when I should report. My crew was waiting and Buddy smiled, "I thought you got cold feet and we might have to go looking for you. We're going to help down at Dak Tu. They are being hit hard and need some Medevac help. It will give you the opportunity to familiarize yourself with our bird."

I grabbed my gear I had stored in a locker at Operations, and then we headed out the flight line. Lieutenant Riley again, went over the emergency procedures and location of the equipment. As he did, Captain Atkins sat in the cockpit and started his preflight checklist. Lieutenant Riley joined him and when the engines started, Burkowitz (Burky), closed the side cargo door. He pointed to a jump seat and said, "Doc, strap and plug in."

When I plugged in my headset, I recognized the more sophisticated communication system. There was not as much of the static background noise and maybe it was my imagination, but communicating was easier.

I was use to Billy's aggressive take offs. Buddy increased the speed of our bird and raised to ten feet, hovered, raised to twenty feet, hovered again, he got finale clearance from the tower, and then dropped the nose, kicked in the engines and we were off. We contacted Detachment 1 and they gave us coordinates for our Medevac pickup. We were there within twenty minutes.

I was use to Sammy and Julio loading the wounded. Now, Burky and I did the loading. With the Pedro, you loaded from the rear. You had to exit the aircraft, drop the rear webbing, load your two litters, and strap them in. When we loaded a third, there was no place for Burky and I to sit. We would kneel behind the cockpit.

I was use to the Medevac's out of Pleiku. With the Pedro, any fighting was off in the distance and it was safe for us to land and exit the aircraft. We were retrieving two patients; the Army Medic said both needed IV's started. I asked Buddy, if we had time to get the IV's going. He said, "All that is required is let me know how much time you need. Unless for our safety we need to leave, you do everything required to save those men."

I got both IV's started, changed a dressing on one man, and gave Buddy the signal we were ready. We arrived at Pleiku in a matter of minutes and unloaded our patients to the waiting ambulance. I was expecting us to go back out. When we did not, Riley told me the Medevac area had become unsafe and we would wait until things calmed down.

Chapter Eleven

While waiting on the flight line at Pleiku, it disappointed me when I could not find my previous flight crew. When I walked back, Buddy told me we had a rescue mission. Our bird was being checked out and refueled. I jumped onboard and rechecked my equipment and backpack.

The Pedro's rescue hydraulic wench system mounted outside and above the right side door. When Riley showed me the equipment used on the Pedro, he showed me a new device called the Penetrator. We used the Penetrator to help in areas of dense foliage as opposed to the horse color, which often tangeled. They made the Penetrator of steel and it had spring-loaded seats, which opened in a triangular configuration. There were straps for the patient and you. After strapping the patient and yourself, you lifted together. The Penetrator also had a flotation device if the rescue were in water.

Our rescue mission was for a downed Navy F-4 Phantom with a crew of two. Ahead of our arrival were two Phantoms from the down aircraft's squadron, and a Sandy from Pleiku. They had hit the area and they gave us the green light for come in. The rescue area was mountainous with heavy foliage and nowhere to land. This was to be my first rescue using the host system and the Penetrator.

The wreckage was a mile away from the two men who had ejected. They lowered me to check the crew for injuries and then help in their retrieval. Both men were OK except for some minor cuts and bruises. None of the injuries was serious enough to prevent them from using the harness.

I put the co-pilot in the harness first and once he was on board, Burky lowered the cable back down. I got the pilot in the harness and then I jumped on the doughnut and signaled for our retrieval. We had traveled upward only thirty feet when we received incoming gunfire. They were not only shooting at the pilot and me, but they were shooting at our bird.

Buddy yelled, "Hang on — Hang on — I'm climbing to get us out of range. I was looking down and three or four Vietcong were shooting at us. I also noticed one had a grenade launcher he was setting up and aiming in our direction. Suddenly, there was a huge explosion and the cable violently swayed. Buddy, was screaming, "Are you hit — Hang on — We'll get you up." I could also hear Burky yelling something inaudible.

I was holding on to the cable, but between the copter's flight ascension and the explosion, which swung the cable in the opposite direction, there was a loss of tension. I knew ultimately gravity would correct this abnormality and when it did, it could snap the end violently. I looked down to tell the pilot to hold on extra tight when I recognized he was hit by whatever caused the explosion.

His body was missing from the waist down and the harness had the rest of him secured. His fixated eyes appeared to be looking right at me begging for help. I remember the snap of the cable and practically losing my grip. I must have gone into shock, I barely remember getting on board.

My next recollection was talking to a doctor in the emergency room at Da Nang. I had small shrapnel from my knees down, but they barely penetrated the skin. They kept me overnight and then discharged me.

The next day, they removed our crew from the roster. Lieutenant Riley helped me get a ride over to Pleiku to retrieve some of my things from the barracks. That night, I found Jimmy at the NCO club. When I told him of the previous days rescue mission, he said, "Johnson, what the fuck were you doing riding on the donut."

I said, "Good thing I was. If I hadn't, I would not be talking with you now." He gave me a puzzled look. "I was using the Penetrator"

"Shit, I thought you were using the horse collar. Are they any good?"

"Hell yeah, they are a lot easier to use than the horse collar. You don't have to worry about being tangled. It also has a better strap system; makes it easier to strap in with the patient.

The next day, with some of my stuff from the barracks packed in a duffle bag, I got another ride over to Da Nang. When I returned to the barracks, Tom Winters, my roommate was not there. I showered; changed into regular fatigues, hit the mess hall and then the NCO club. After I was there a few minutes, a group invited me to join a table of PJs from the Detachment 7.

I sat drinking my beer and listening to these veterans. I was still in awe of their experiences, confidence, and expertise. I knew I was a novice, but I felt even more incompetent when I was around them. Tom came in while I was sitting there and we later walked back to the barracks. I confessed my feelings of insecurity and he said, "We were all in your shoes at one time. Just watch and learn from us. We all make mistakes, the important thing is to learn from them."

* * *

The few weeks I worked with Detachment 7, when we were on alert or even standby, we rarely went out on rescues. They assigned most rescues to the Jolly Greens because they were armored, faster and could cover longer distances. I found it frustrating at first, then realized I was not getting my butt shot at, so let the other PJs go out. There are always war stories and especially about Pitsenbarger, a PJ who was killed in action. When our team went out, it was a quick retrieval or assisting Medevac.

It was a day our team was standby; they assigned Tom to a Jolly team on alert. The second PJ with him went to sick call and looked as if they were short a man. Captain Atkins said I would be on stand by with the Jolly team. I checked in with the Major who was the Pilot and CO. He called Tom and instructed him to brief me on the Jolly's equipment, and their procedures. We drove out to the flight line and as he went over everything. I realized most days a Jolly Green went out on a mission.

Tom must have been intuitive of my apprehension. He said, "Johnson, don't let the first time get you scared. We don't operate any different than you do on the Pedro. In fact, we have it easier than you do. Our bird is armored and with a larger crew. You will do fine."

That afternoon, we received a call, and we rushed to the flight line. The process of getting in the air with a Jolly Green was slower due to the size of the engines and the checklist. I strapped in, as I listened to the radio chatter, I had not realized we had liftedoff. As with the Huey, the engines were deafening.

I learned our mission was to find a missing Sandy. They gave us the general vicinity, however, the exact time and location he disappeared from radar, was vague. Besides us, three other aircraft were looking. We were flying around one thousand feet in an overlapping pattern. The area was in the highlands. The Sandy had been flying reconnaissance for the Army when it took a hit. He tried to make it back when he went down.

I heard on the radio, "Jolly Green six - three, Bulldog four - four; copy?"

Our co-pilot replied, "Bulldog four - four, Jolly Green six – three, 10-4."

Jolly Green six – three, we have a target." He gave us the coordinates and we changed our heading.

We arrived and spotted the wreckage. As we swept the area and lowered, our hopes for a recovery became pessimistic. There were no landing area nearby, once we felt the area secure, we came in and hovered. Tom dropped in.

Within minutes of being on the ground, Tom radioed, "Jolly Green six - three, PJ - 1. We have no survivor."

"PJ—1, Roger that"

Jolly Green six - three, Send PJ-2 with a bag."

"PJ—1, 10-4"

I strapped in carrying the body bag and they lowered me. I joined Tom at the wreckage. The pilot was still onboard and it appeared he did not have time to bail. It also appeared he had died instantly. We pulled him out of cockpit, placed him the bag, zipped it closed and carried it to the retrieval area. We placed the pilot in a lowered litter basket and he was lifted. They lowered a Penetrator for Tom and me. It was a quiet ride back to base.

* * *

It did not look to bother the rest of my crew when all we were doing were medevac; I wanted more. They called us again for medevac out in the highlands near the DMZ. We were within 20 minutes of our target area, when I heard Buddy say, "Damn, what was that?" I felt our engine falter. Buddy said, "Hold on guys, we might have lost our engine." I felt the aircraft shudder.

Lieutenant Riley radioed, "Da Nang control, Rescue 4 – 4; we have an emergency"

"Rescue 4-4, Da Nang control; say again."

"Da Nang Control, We have lost our engine and are going down. We are declaring an emergency. Mayday. Rescue 4 – 4 Mayday, Mayday."

As our bird continued to shake, but, it did not lose complete power. Buddy appeared to have control, yet we were on a quick decent. The greatest fear most have with helicopter flying is loss of engine and maneuverability. Very few survive. For whatever reason, I did not panic.

Even with our quick decent, Buddy found a clearing large enough for us to land. We felt as if we glided more like an airplane than a helicopter decent, yet when we hit, it was a heavy thud, which shook the aircraft.

Buddy yelled, "Anyone hurt?"

Luckily, no one was hurt. We unbuckled and before we left our bird, everyone grabbed a weapon. Burkowitz and I opened the weapons locker and grabbed an M-16 with an extra clip. After a cautious inspection of the area, we stepped out.

I stood watch as Buddy and Burkowitz climbed up to inspect the engine. Lieutenant Riley radioed Da Nang Control we had landed without incident or injury to the crew. As soon as they opened the engine cover, they realized our mechanical problem; our fuel pump and line was damaged. In addition, the left rear-landing strut was damaged, but still holding the weight. Again, Lieutenant Riley notified Da Nang of our assessment. They notified us they would send another unit with a mechanic and parts. They gave us no ETA.

Although we were in a clearing, there were hills, and a heavy jungle around us. Had the enemy been in our area, we were an easy target. We all agreed that we would be safer hiding in the jungle than sitting out in the open. We moved so we could still have a view of our bird.

Within the hour, we heard someone moving towards us. My heart was banging as I had my rifle pointed where we expected the VC. When the group reached the clearing, only one man stepped out surveying the area and our bird. He then ducked backin.

We next heard, "Anyone here? U.S. Marines over here. Are you injured?"

Lieutenant Riley yelled, "U.S. Air Force Flight Crew — no—we are fine."

Captain Atkins whispered, "Sergeant Burkowitz, I want you to move forward and cover us until we can get a visual." Burkowitz nodded and moved toward the clearing, his gun held in the ready position.

We watched from across the clearing, first one, then two, and finally ten Marines walk out into the clearing. I joined our crew in sighing in relief. We walked out to meet the Marine patrol lead by a sergeant. He stated, they saw us go down, and headed in our direction. The sergeant said, "We haven't seen any VC in this area for a few days, but we had a minor encounter with a group last week. Our unit has a camp about two klicks from here. I think you would be safer there."

Captain Atkins agreed and before we left, we notified Da Nang Command of our move to their camp. Da Nang still did not give us an ETA. I grabbed my backpack, plugged my helmet headset into the radio, and followed the group back into the jungle.

Our walk took us over an hour as the Sergeant had us moving in a zigzagging direction. The location of the Marine's camp was on an elevated hill where they had a 360-degree view of the surrounding area. The majority of the trees were removed and used for constructing watchtowers and other temporary shelters. It looked as if it was a well-fortified camp. All the shelters were dug into the ground with tree and other vegetative roofs. This camp was part of a division secured this camp plus two more. There were forty marines posted there.

Their commanding officer was a captain with a second lieutenant as second in command. They welcomed us, showed us their facilities, and then they took us to their mobile mess hall. We were feed and then shown to our temporary quarters.

I kept my helmet on to monitor the radio; however, that evening they told us they were in contact with Da Nang Command and they had men that would monitor the radio during the night. I saved my battery and turned it off.

That night, we were feed a great meal, sat in what they called their club, and had a few drinks before retiring for the evening. The next morning, Da Nang Command notified us they would have a crew out to either fix our bird or return us to Da Nang. We thanked our host before we left their camp.

The Marine second lieutenant assigned a patrol of eight men to escort us back and stand watch until we left. We zigzagged again in a slow movement to our bird's location. We waited for two hours in the edge of the jungle before we heard the incoming helicopter. It was one of our squadron's Jolly Greens, with two mechanics on board.

I was monitoring our radio when I heard, "Pedro 7 – 7, Jolly 8-4, copy?"

I responded, "Jolly 8-4, Pedro 7 – 7, 10-4."

"Pedro 7 – 7, you got room for us to put down?"

Before I responded, I asked Captain Atkins, "Jolly 8-4 want to know if there is enough room for them to land."

Buddy said, "They have more than enough."

I radioed, "Jolly 8-4, you are a go for landing."

"Pedro 7-7, roger that."

We walked out with the Marines first. The Marine patrol stayed guarding the area as the mechanics changed our fuel pump and replaced the fuel lines. They started nd tested our bird. When a full system checked, we thanked our guards, got on board, lifted, and followed Jolly 8-4 back to Da Nang.

* * *

It was in February, my flight crew, Pedro 7-7, went on Rest and Recuperation (R & R). Since I had only been in Vietnam since December, I was ineligible for R & R. They sent me back to Pleiku and told my Pedro crew they were assigned to Plieku when they returned. Instead of going back to the Army flight crew with Billy and Larry, They temporarily assigned me to the hospital surgical area.

From the beginning, we were doing marathon surgeries. After the second day working with the same surgeon, we were 18 hours into our shift, and it appeared we were nowhere close to stopping. I was falling asleep on my feet and he kept yelling at me to get my attention.

Between patients, he gave me a pill. "Look, I take this stuff to stay alert, and function. You will notice as if you have had a couple cups of strong coffee and plenty of energy." I was so tired; I did not resist and took it. It was not long before I had an abundance of energy.

A few days later, I was in another marathon surgery. I happened to be working with the same surgeon and I asked him for another pill. He gave me one and a prescription. He also gave me a second prescription, which would allow me to sleep. I later found out most of the doctors who worked these long shifts were using one type of drug or another. They were also supplying their assistants with some of the same drugs.

When using these drugs, I never felt out of control or intoxicated like with alcohol or weed. I always felt alert, efficient, and able to function. However, by using these drugs regularly, I required an increase in the dosage to obtain the same effects. I did not give it any thought; it was something I, and so many others did.

* * *

On top of all the hours in surgery and flight missions, a rotational list had two doctors and medics going out into the neighboring villages treating the Vietnamese. It was for vaccinations for smallpox, diphtheria, etc. The doctors would do exams and treat most things they found. However, we did no surgical procedures other than something minor.

One week my name came up and ironically, Jimmy's did too. The morning came and we loaded the supplies into the back of a jeep ambulance. They assigned a driver and two Army guards and off we went to a village about a twenty-minute drive from the base.

It was a tiny village with only twenty huts; it was a farming community with no commercial buildings. Jimmy, along with the doctor he assisted, used a hut at one end of the village; my assigned doctor and I were at the other end. As soon as we set up, the Vietnamese got in line. It was women and children with a few elderly males.

We worked for over two hours when the lines were getting smaller. We took a break and Jimmy and I stood talking, "Hell this is a lot easier than working in the hospital. Maybe we should volunteer to do this more often," I laughed.

"Yeah, and the hours are a lot better," Jimmy said. After our break, we returned to our respective hut.

All of sudden there was a loud deafening explosion coming from the other end of the village. All I could see was smoke and dust rising from what looked like the hut Jimmy and the doctor were working. There were screams coming from the Vietnamese as they ran from the scene. Instinctively the doctor and I ran toward the location.

When we arrived, I could not believe what I was seeing. There were blood and body parts all over and the hut was smoldering. On the ground in front of the hut, lay Jimmy, with an arm missing, his abdomen ripped open, and his organs spilled out. Even before I reached him, I knew he was dead. Automatically we checked him; however, we found no pulse, and his eyes fixated.

Inside laid the doctor with his clothing smoldering. Most of his body had burns and lacerations. He was alive, but we needed to get him to the hospital. We started an IV and covered the worse of the injuries with bandages. We then loaded him and Jimmy's remains in the ambulance and started the rush back for the base.

I was in denial and I could not believe this nightmare. Jimmy's doctor was semi-conscious, in severe pain and we injected him with the only vial of morphine available. I tried to focus my attention on the doctor; however, my eyes kept turning to the blood soaked sheet covering Jimmy. How the hell could this have happened?

We hit the entrance to the base with the siren blaring. They waved us through security, and we never stopped until we screeched in front of the emergency room. I remember no one calling ahead, but there were two doctors and several medics waiting. I jumped out, helped load the doctor onto a gurney, and then pushed him into the emergency room. The ER doctors took over; I was pushed out of the room.

They escorted my doctor and me to a small office and told to wait. Within minutes, an Army Major and a Sergeant came in and asked questions. At first, I was still in shock and was having trouble remembering the events and in what order they occurred.

Between the two of us, we could account for what we had seen and heard. We did not know what had happened other than something had exploded.

Even with the security interview completed, we were still in denial. We sat there looking at each other. One of the emergency room doctors came in and told us they took the doctor to surgery. Although he had multiple lacerations, the burns were the worst of his injuries. They expected doing what they could to stabilize him and then airlift him to a burn center back in the US. Tragically, he never left Pleiku alive. The ER doctor asked, "You guys okay?" We both replied yes. "Let's make sure. Come with me and let me have a look."

The ER doctor had me undress and did a quick check for injuries. Until I undressed, I had not realized my fatigues were soaked in blood. I told the ER doctor Jimmy and I were good friends. "We trained for Pararescue together. We were both stationed at Lackland before coming here. Tell me it didn't happen."

I returned to my barracks and was taking a shower when I realized I was sobbing. I could not stop and stood under the shower trying to hide my uncontrolled emotions. When I recovered, I dressed and went to the NCO Club. I ordered something to drink, however, after a sip I became nauseated. I returned to the barracks. As soon as I closed the door to my room, the sobbing started again.

I cried myself to sleep and woke up the next morning still in denial. How could this have happened?

A few days later, I found out the Army sent a patrol back to the village. They questioned several of the Vietnamese. The witnesses stated a Vietnamese female approached Jimmy with a baby. When she handed the baby to him, she ran the other way. Within seconds, there was the explosion, which killed Jimmy and critically injured the doctor. It was a hand grenade attached to the baby the source of the explosion.

They gave me a day off and then I returned to surgery. Several days later, I had returned to my barracks after a marathon of surgery. I heard a knock on my door and when I answered, two of Jimmy's and my drinking buddies were waiting. As they sat on the bed, the three of us were trying to understand and make sense of our loss. They told me Jimmy's personal effects were boxed and sent to his home in Houston. Somehow, they overlooked his beret and jump wings. One said, "We did not know what to do with them. We thought maybe you would take them and when you returned to Texas, you could give them to his family."

My eyes teared and I said. "Thank you guys. It would be a crime if his beret and wings did not make it home. Nothing would make me prouder than to present them to his family." Several months later, I did.

I joined my drinking buddies at the NCO Club. We spent the evening sharing our personal relationship with Jimmy and drinking toast after toast to our lost friend. I have no idea how long we stayed or how much alcohol we consumed. All I remember was I was feeling no pain and as I lay in my bed watching the room spin, I said to no one, "I've got six months, two weeks, four days, and a wake up." I did not know how accurate it was, but it seemed right.

Chapter Twelve

After the two weeks when my Pedro team returned from R & R, I again packed my duffle bag and returned to Da Nang. With Jimmy's death, it did not matter where they stationed me. I was mourning and I felt my life would never be the same. Jimmy had often said I was someone he could always count on. I felt the same; he was my rock when the crazy world was incomprehensible. I kept asking myself how I would survive over here without him.

The first night back at Da Nang AFB, I sat at the NCO Club and told Tom of my loss. Even when I felt embarrassed in front of Tom and the other PJs, I could not hold back the tears. Tom offered no consoling guidance; although I saw in his eyes, he understood my grief. Again, I sat and drowned my sorrow with alcohol.

The next day my crew was on standby. After, breakfast I reported to the command operations and checked in with Captain

Atkins. The crew was relaxed from their R & R. They had heard of Jimmy's death and each offered their condolences. I found it hard to listen to their adventuresome R & R stories. I kept going outside to be alone.

Colonel Price's aide came and said the colonel wanted to see to me. Walking to his office, I expected he too would offer his condolences. When he asked me to sit, it was a surprise. He said. "Sergeant Johnson, I understand you lost a buddy last week. I am sorry for your loss—but—I am told you are letting your grief get the better of you. I have an operation to run and I can't allow anyone to jeopardize its' effectiveness. Do you understand?"

"Yes, Sir." I felt myself stiffen and sweat breakout on my forehead.

He said, "Are you married?"

"Yes, Sir."

"We give married men more time for R & R if they wish to meet their wives in Hawaii. I would recommend you avail yourself of the option and spend quality time with your wife."

I replied, "Thank you, sir. My wife is in the Air Force and stationed at Wilford Hall. Yes, if it can be arranged, I would prefer to spend my R & R with my wife. We just got married last May."

"That's good. My aide will help you make the arrangements. I will contact your wife's CO and request she receives immediate leave. I am allowing your R & R just as soon as the arrangements are made. Until your return from R & R, I am pulling you off the rotation. I expect you to return ready to do your job. Do we understand each other?"

"Yes, Sir."

"Dismissed."

I stood, saluted, and left his office. When I returned to the readiness room, Lieutenant Riley pulled me aside. I told him what the colonel had said, he interrupted, "Wait a minute I want Buddy to hear this."

Buddy joined us; I repeated what the colonel had said. I finished by telling them the colonel had pulled me from the duty roster. Buddy said, "The heartless son-of-a-bitch." He paused, looked at me, and asked, "Do you feel impaired to handle any mission they might throw at us?"

"No, Sir, I will be fine. I agree with the colonel, spending time with my wife would help my mood."

Riley asked, "How long you been here?"

"Five months."

Buddy said, "Yeah, they wait until you been here at least six months before allowing R & R." I could tell Buddy was not happy. If I could not go on missions or while gone, he would be short his PJ. He would have to double down on another PJ, and it would make it difficult for them. He said, "It's up to you, if you are okay, I will go talk to the colonel and get you reinstated."

"Thank you Buddy, but it would do me good to get away." Although he differed, he respected my decision. I felt ashamed I had let my grief for Jimmy affect my ability to do my job.

The next day, I went over to base communications, I could contact Genie by MARS (Military Auxillary Radio System). It was hard to hear each other, but she was excited meeting me in Hawaii. It was comforting to hear her voice. I had not taken the time to write her of Jimmy's death. When I told her, I heard her break down and cry. Shortly after telling her, we lost our connection. The radio operator said he would try to contact her later. I left a written message for him to convey.

* * *

It took a week to complete the arrangements, and then I caught a flight over to Clark AFB in the Philippines. My next hop was to Hickam AFB in Hawaii onboard a C-141. On the flight, there were a dozen men going on R & R. In addition, the rear contained the haunting black bags. With the lost heroes onboard, it was hard to get excited over my R & R.

Once at Hickam, I caught a military bus over to Honolulu. Genie was at the hotel and waiting in the lobby. Just as when we separated, she was holding me tight and sobbing. The difference, I was crying with her.

We stayed in a hotel on the beach. The first 24 hours, I slept most of it. It had taken me 36 hours to reach my destination. During the day, we did shopping, touring of Honolulu, walked and laid on the beach. We took a tourist excursion to Pearl Harbor and the USS Arizona Memorial. Most nights we ate at the hotel, had numerous drinks at the bar on the beach and ended with a romantic evening in our room.

Jimmy's death, at the beginning, was the center of our conversation. I listened to Dad's advice and did not hold back any details; however, I most likely was too graphic. I saw Genie's fear and apprehension for my safety grow. She asked questions and I would lie to avoid telling her what was going on.

After three days avoiding and being untruthful to her, she caught me in my own lies. I said, "Genie, I love you too much and I don't want you worrying. Besides, many things I do are classified (it was not a lie). When I return, maybe I'll tell you. Until then, please just don't ask me, and then I won't have to lie to you." She stopped asking questions and we stopped talking about Vietnam.

Genie told me she had moved from the apartment we had before. There were problems with the maintenance and they raised the rent. Paul, Kathy and her found a place for a small increase in the rent. It was further away from the base, but she said the apartments were bigger and the grounds, pool, etc. were also nicer.

We parted in Hawaii, with Genie in tears and I in anger knowing what awaited me. Once onboard, our military flight returning to Vietnam, I worked on my mood. I convinced myself, I needed to keep my head in the game to make it safely home. I could not and would not allow myself affected by the shit I experienced. I had a team who expected me to carry my weight and I would not let them down. It required I stay sharp to perform my rescue duties and save lives. I had taken an oath when I became a PJ and I would uphold it. By the time I reached Da Nang, I was prepared to handle whatever they threw at me.

* * *

Upon my return to Da Nang, I checked in first at personnel, then went to the 38th ARRS Detachment 7 Operations, and checked in with them. I could not believe the changes in two weeks. There had been scuttlebutt, they would replace our HH-3E with HH-53B or Super Jolly Greens. We had one Super Jolly, now we had nothing but Super Jolly's.

They transferred Captain Atkins and my crew to Bien Hoa AFB to Detachment 6. The only Pedro left at Da Nang they used for any emergencies at the base, crashes involving fire. They reassigned me to a new Super Jolly Green (HH-53B) with the call name "Jolly 9-7". My new CO and pilot was Major Larry Hicks, second in command and co-pilot was Captain William (Willy) Blair, Flight Engineer was Sergeant Bill Sands, and the first PJ was Technical Sergeant Charles (Charlie) Kiesler. I was the second PJ.

When I checked in, my new crew had just rotated off alert status. My roommate Tom Winters was on standby. He was pleased to see me and we sat in the ready room while he told me of the new changes. He told me Charlie Kiesler had been in the class ahead of him and this was his second tour. He described him as easy going and well experienced. He thought I would get along with him. He said Major Hicks was one of the best Jolly pilots, yet they called him 'Crazy Larry'. He did not know Captain Blair or Sergeant Sands other to recognize them.

While things were quiet, we went over to the flight line and he showed me the new Super Jolly Greens. They had the latest and greatest communication systems. I found headset jacks throughout the cargo area, making it possible to be in any area and still communicate with the cockpit. He told me it had Doppler radar to detect SAM's. I did not understand how sophisticated or even what Doppler radar was. The cargo area was larger giving it increased capacity to carry troop, litters, and cargo. However, for ARRS usage of the Super Jolly over predecessor was its fueling probe and external fuel tanks. These add-ons would increase the flight distance capabilities. In addition, the steel armament plating on the aircraft was superior to its predecessor. The engines were larger, although, the speed was not much different. The guns were the same. Additional cable length improved the host system, which they mounted right above the right door.

* * *

My first flight with my new crew was three days after I had returned. We flew, as the backup to Jolly 5-6 and our mission was to recover the two pilots of a Phantom F-4 (call sign Popeye) from Cam Ranh Bay. Both the pilot and co-pilot of the Phantom had jettisoned safety when their engines caught fire. However, both men tangled their parachutes in trees. There was a Sandy (A-3), keeping watch, and running interference. Command advised both men to stay hidden in the trees until recovery could arrive.

While the lead Jolly, circled to ensure there were no hostiles in the area, we made a wider circle doing the same thing. I heard, "Jolly five - six, Sandy two -five, copy?"

"Sandy two - five, Jolly five - six, 10-4"

"Jolly five - six, you've got a green light on recover. Popeye 1 & 2 are—" he continued giving the coordinates.

"Popeye -1, Jolly five - six, Copy?"

Jolly five - six, Popeye -1, I'm caught up in the trees, can't get loose."

"Popeye 1, Roger that. Are you injured? How about Popeye -2?"

The radio chatter continued with the Phantom pilot telling the lead Jolly they had no injuries, but they were hung up in the trees. The Jolly continue to circle as he lowered to get in position for the recovery operation. The next thing we heard was the lead Jolly radio an emergency.

"Da Nang control, Jolly five - six. We have a red light on our hydraulics and a visual. We are losing pressure. I say again, we have a red light and we are returning to base."

"Jolly five - six, Da Nang control, are you declaring an emergency?"

The lead Jolly changed radio frequency and they limped back towards Da Nang AFB. Fortunately, there were no injuries and damage to the helicopter was minimal. Detachment 7 Command, radioed us to take over the recovery. Maj. Hicks radioed, "Popeye - 1, Jolly nine - seven, Copy?

Jolly nine - seven, Popeye -1 here, Get us the hell out of here."

"Popeye -1, Roger that."

We moved into position hovering over the co-pilot first. We lowered the Penetrator, gave him instruction how to open it up and strap in. We raised him up and moved over to the pilot. However, the pilot's recovery was not so easy.

The pilot yelled, "Jolly, you got to get me out. My balls are about to burst." His response confused us, but we could not help but laugh.

Major Hicks replied, "Popeye – 1, What's the problem? Are you injured"?

"Jolly—I will be if you don't get me out. I've got a fucking tree limb caught up in my strap and it's crushing my balls." Now we are hysterically laughing. But, it was not a joke.

I volunteered to go down. Charlie handed me a 12-inch knife. He said, "Careful with it, its razor sharp."

As I reached the pilot, I found him tangled in not only his straps, but the cords of the parachute too. I had unstrapped from the

Penetrator, was hanging in the tree, and cut the cords as I worked my way towards the pilot. He was yelling at me to hurry. When I got to him, he had a large limb he had impaled between himself and the straps. The only way to release him was to cut the branch. I took five minutes to cut through the limb enough to break it off and release the pilot from his confinement. They lowered the penetrator, I strapped us in, and we were brought up at the same time Major Hicks gained altitude.

As we were returning, the Phantom's co-pilot asked his flight commander, "Does this mean our new call name is now Olive Oyl?"

* * *

The routine picked up. We worked two days and off one. With the new Super Jolly's we could cover larger areas; hence, we were covering for more Air Force bases and Army units. Most were normal recoveries while there were the occasional tedious and dangerous ones.

My focus was to restore what I had perceived as a deficit in my status among my peer PJs. After Jimmy's death, I always felt Tom Winters went to someone about my emotional breakdown. I determined I would not show any weakness. I watched and learned from Charlie. I picked his brain on everything I felt doubtful. On days off, I would join other PJs in running 5 miles and doing the usual calisthenics.

I did not put myself at additional risk, although when required Charlie or me to drop in, I would volunteer. With the new Penetrator, unless the injured individual was unable, we allowed them to strap in and we stayed onboard. Medical procedures when required where done onboard.

What was missing; was the personal camaraderie I experienced with the other two teams. This team was all business, especially the two officers. The enlisted men did not call them by their first names. Major Hicks was less formal; he would often tease and attempt to keep things light. While Captain Blair was, "Yes Sir and No Sir." Bill Sands and Charlie Kiesler were sociable and especially conscience of working as a team. Once Bill and Charlie left the aircraft or the command center, they did not socialize with me. They had their own friends and agenda and they never asked me to join.

Of the 12 PJs at Detachment 7, three were like me, just out of the Pipeline. Of the three, I became friendly with Mike Ellison who I had crossed paths during the Pipeline days. He was at Keesler AFB near Biloxi, Mississippi. They assigned Mike to a team who rotated with mine. Although Mike and I were not in the same barracks, we hung out together and often got sloppy drunk at the NCO Club. It was infrequent Tom Winters, who remained my roommate in the barracks, and I was off at the same time. I liked Tom, but I did not trust him. If we crossed paths, we remained friendly.

In my private moments, my thoughts would return to the friendship I had with Jimmy. We had been each other's support through the Pipeline and then over here. When overwhelmed by the horridness of this war, he could always distract me. Jimmy could find humor in anything and made light of the dreariness. How I wished I could somehow reverse the awfulness of his death. As much as I grieved when alone, I would not allow others to see it.

Chapter Thirteen

It was November and we were back into the Monsoon season with all the rain. It was a constant fight to keep your equipment and supplies dry. It was impossible to keep yourself dry. Patience was low and tempers often surged. It took extra effort to concentrate on my duties and not succumb to weather.

It was my team's rotation to alert status and it was mid-morning when we received notice a B-52 was hit by suspected SAMs (surface-to-air missile). Our team took the lead and the second Jolly team flew as our backup. When we were scrambled, our mission involving a B-52 and its possible location was classified. Once airborne, Major Hicks they gave him the information. The aircraft had been on a bombing run over Hanoi and was down somewhere near the DMZ (de-militarized zone).

They scrambled Navy fighter jets from the Carrier Constellation. They had picked up the B-52's emergency beacon, although, they could not make radio contact. We did not know if the bomber crew had survived. The reports showed it had taken a direct hit. The surveillance aircraft in the area were reporting enemy ground moving towards the target area. They were also getting warning signals of potential SAMs. We knew this would be a tedious and dangerous mission.

Both our team and our backup were flying together when we picked up the emergency beacon on the down aircraft. We took the lead and moved in closer to the signal while our backup flew a wide circle around the target area. We homed in on the signal making our circles tighter, our altitude lower, as the signal got stronger.

Bill Sands was at the left, Charlie Kiesler had the right, and I had the read cargo door. All doors were open while we manned the machine guns. All of a sudden, Bill yelled, "Target at eight o'clock." As we passed, I could see the wreckage. It appeared the bomber broke up when it hit and the debris field was at least two hundred yards. However, the fuselage appeared to be intact.

Major Hicks was on the radio, "Detachment 7–Command, Jolly nine - seven, copy?"

"Command, Jolly nine - seven, go ahead."

"We located the target." Command directed us to pull out and let the Fighter jets from the carrier make a pass clearing any potential hostiles. We lifted to 1,000 ft. and widened our circle. Just as we hit our altitude, from the rear door, I watched two Phantoms swoop in drop two bombs each and a line of gunfire to both sides of the wreckage. It was impressive and I thought no one could have survived.

"Jolly nine - seven, Pluto two - zero, copy?"

Captain Blair replied, "Pluto two - zero, 10-4."

"Jolly, you're a go for deployment. We got your back."

"Pluto two - zero, Roger that."

We returned making our decent and tightening our circle. Major Hicks said, "Head's up, I'm taking us in." As Major Hicks got us down to around one hundred feet and after our second pass over the area, we drew arms fire. Bill and Charlie spotted the location and returned fire. Captain Blair had me move forward and he shut the rear door for the aircraft and crew's protection.

Major Hicks made two more passes while Bill and Charlie fired their guns. On the second pass, I spotted a man crawling out of the bushes and he was waving something white.

I yelled, "Got a survivor at five o'clock."

Captain Blair said, "PJ-2, we need to make this fast. Get ready."

I checked my backpack, unhooked my flight helmet from the aircraft communication system, and hooked it into my backpack radio. Although I carried a 45 sidearm, I grabbed an M-16 and two extra clips from the locker. I called out, "PJ-2, ready."

With Bill and Charlie watching the tree lines, Major Hicks brought our bird in and hovered 6 feet, while I jumped out the right door. As soon as I hit the ground, I was running for the area that I had seen the survivor.

I heard Captain Blair, "PJ-2, we are pulling up to a safer altitude."

I said, "Jolly nine - seven, Roger that." I had not run 50 ft. when I heard gunfire. I hit the deck and saw the incoming fire's location, however, they were not shooting at me, they were shooting at my bird. It appeared they had hit it several times. I radioed, "Jolly, You get hit?" However, I did not get a response. I listened to Major Hick pull the bird up and out of the area. Within a minute, I could not hear the bird at all.

I crawled into the brush looking for the survivor. I could not find him. Whispering, I said, "Where are you? Are you hurt?" I crawled a few feet and then called out to him again.

After a couple minutes, I heard a whisper, "Over here." When I found him, he put his fingers up to his lips and pointed over to his left. I could now hear several people moving around in the brush. I noticed that on his flight suit his name was Crowley. We sat holding our breath, hoping they would not find us. Crowley had his pistol in his hand and I had my M-16 ready with the safety off. I couldn't hear anything but the banging of my heart. The sweat poured down my face.

We sat in silence for what seemed like hours hearing the men working their way through the brush. At one point, they were within thirty feet from us and then they moved away. When we could no longer hear them, Crowley whispered, "I'm glad to see you. I thought there for a minute, they would find us."

"Me too," I said. "Now, are you injured?"

"Yeah, I broke my leg and I'm bleeding from somewhere. By the way, I'm Colonel Thomas Crowley"

"Glad to meet you, Colonel, I'm Sergeant Ken Johnson. I'm a PJ from the 38th rescue squadron at Da Nang."

I checked him out and verified he broke his right leg. It was not a severe or compound fracture, but the fibula of the right leg broke. I found a deep cut on his right shoulder; the whole back of his flight suit was bloody. I checked the rest of him and he had scratches and bruises. I pulled my backpack off, and I put a compression bandage on his shoulder. I found an inflatable splint, opened the package, and then slid it over his lower leg. I told the colonel. "Hang on, I'm inflating the splint. It will hurt like hell." When I inflated it, his face went red but he did not scream.

I asked, "Where is the rest of your crew?"

"We went down hard. I'm the only one who survived."

"Colonel, we will make a run for the copter. I will put you in a harness and then they will hoist us up. I think it will be too painful for you to stand on the leg. We will crawl to the edge of the brush.

Once we are in the open, I want you to get on my back and I'll carry you." He gave me an affirmative nod. "I can give you something for the pain, but if you can tolerate it, I would rather have you alert until we get onboard. You think you can tolerate the pain a while longer?"

He was sweating and I could tell the pain was intolerable. "Yeah, I think so."

I still did not know if the VC was anywhere close, but I had to take the chance. In a whisper, I said, "Jolly nine - seven, PJ-2, Copy?" I heard nothing. A little louder this time, "Jolly nine - seven, PJ-2, Copy?"

Before I could call a third time, Colonel Crowley said, "I don't think it's a good idea getting too loud. We still might have company."

I looked at him and offered an alternative. "Okay, I will try tapping the mike, and see if I get a response." I tapped out SOS on the mike and waited. I tried again and got no response. I looked at my watch and I had been on the ground an hour and a half.

I said, "Colonel when they dropped me off, I think I saw my bird take a couple hits. If they did, they may have had to return to base. Our backup bird should still be in the area. I'll call them."

The Colonel gave me an anxious look before he spoke. "Doc, I'm concerned this radio chatter might bring attention to us. It could make any rescue team a target."

"Colonel, to be honest with you, I wasn't planning on spending any time here. Let me see if I can our butts out of here."

I changed my radio to the emergency channel. "Jolly five - six, PJ-2, Copy"

I must have called a dozen times when I got a response. "PJ-2, Spotted Eagle, copy?"

I got excited, "Spotted Eagle, PJ-2, 10-4"

"PJ-2, Command directive is for radio silence. Enemy movement in your area, copy?"

"Spotted Eagle, Roger that. Thanks." I turned to the Colonel. "I just got a response from Spotted Eagle. I think he might be a fighter jet. He said, stay put and they would be back ASAP."

"Yeah, I know Spotted Eagle. He is a naval F-4, I think from the carrier Constellation."

When we settled in he said, "How about you call me Tom. We can forget the rank stuff for now."

"Okay, Tom, what survival gear do you carry on board your aircraft?"

Tom said, "If not destroyed, there will be five days of rations for each crew member. Normal crew is five, but we only had four on this run."

"I want to explore our area. This isn't a bad place, but let me see if I can find a more comfortable place. I'll wait until dark and then go explore the wreckage and bring back anything we can use."

I crawled around in a circle for one hundred yards from where I had left Tom. The brush was thick and the terrain rough. I found a small stream where the water moved, which would be a source if we needed it.

When I returned, I told Tom what I found. "There isn't an area close that is any better. So let's stay here." He agreed. I could also tell the leg was being intolerable. "It looks like we might be here overnight. I will give you something for the pain. I'll also let air out of the splint. It should give you relief too." When I finished, the morphine did its job and he was asleep within ten minutes.

He had lost a bunch of blood from the deep cut on his shoulder. I had one IV kit, and while he was asleep, I hooked him up and gave him IV fluids. Then I cleaned and redressed the cut.

The mosquitoes in this brushy area were wicked. I took mud and smeared it on Tom's exposed skin and then on mine. I sat waiting and listening for any sounds of enemy movement in our area. I heard nothing but birds and small animals.

When it got dark, Tom was still asleep. I made my way over to the fuselage. When I first crawled in, I found two dead bodies. I was not ready for it. I knew there was one more and I finally found it. I said aloud, "Ok, no more surprises. Let's find what I came here for and get out." I forgot to ask Tom the exact location of the survival items. I had a brought a small pin light from my pack. Using the light, I found two packs of C rations in an attached pocket under the pilot and co-pilot's seats. I also spotted an inflatable raft. I looked and found several compartments in the back of the cockpit. To get access, I had to move one body.

Still talking out-loud to myself, "Holy — Shit. Why are these bodies spooking me? Okay, I got meals for at least five days and rain gear I can use as shelter. What else do I need? Come on—think." I turned the pin light off. I convinced myself I had enough for tonight, after all, someone would be back for us tomorrow.

When I returned, Tom was still asleep. I covered him with the poncho and then pulled one over me thinking I might get a little sleep, but never could. I found out making a canopy with the poncho, the mosquitoes would leave me alone.

* * *

The next day, Tom and I traded wearing my helmet and listening for any radio communication. While he listened, I napped. We also heard no VC in our area. We had the C-rations and I made trips to the stream to retrieve water for us. Towards the end of the day, his pain was getting unbearable and I gave him another dose of Morphine. As before, within minutes, he was asleep and again he slept the night. I slept but woke up when it rained. I got Tom covered under the poncho and I crawled under the other. I tried to nap until it was light.

We sat for two days with no communication, I said, "I will go back to the aircraft and get more C-rations. I found what we had under the pilot and co-pilot's seats. Where would I find the others?"

Tom said, "You remember where you found the rain gear? Look in the compartments in that area. You should find any of the survival gear, first-aid supplies, and more C-rations."

I waited until dusk hoping I could get in and out before it got dark. When I approached the aircraft, the stench of the dead bodies was so strong I did not know if I could go inside. By tying my handkerchief over my nose, I could tolerate the stench, although, it was nauseating. I found what I was looking for and returned.

When I got back, Tom wrinkled his nose, "What's that smell?"

"The men in the aircraft are decomposing. The odor was strong, it must have got on my clothes."

He said, "You got to do something. You really stink."

I crawled to the stream, rinsed my clothes, and washed. I hung my clothes in the bushes and wore the poncho.

* * *

The days and nights ran together and even though we were listening, we heard nothing on the radio. We both wanted to break radio silence but knew doing so might bring the VC back to our area.

It was day six or seven we heard bombing off in the distance. At night, we heard the sounds of the bombing and we see the flashes as they went off.

I didn't know how much longer we might be here and we were low on C-rations. I said, "I will do more exploring today. I want to see if I can find us food somewhere."

To camouflage myself, I smeared mud on my face. I left my backpack with Tom. I walked along the bank of the stream thinking if there was a farming village nearby it would be near the water source. I was not wrong.

There was a small village of ten huts located five miles from the crash site. They had two cooking fires. I saw two men, a dozen women, and children. I watched several of the women go to a small barrel and scoop what looked like rice. They took it over and put it into whatever they were cooking.

I planned to sneak into the village after everyone was asleep, get the rice and anything left in the pots they were cooking. I moved a short distance back upstream and I was lying on the side of the bank waiting for it to get dark.

Suddenly, I heard this noise above me on the bank. My heart was racing and I pulled my pistol. Over the bank, came a dog. He did not bark or make any noise, but just stopped by the stream looked at me and wagged his tail. That was all I needed for the dog to bark, so I whispered to him trying to coax him. He did not act as if he feared me; he came over and let me pet him. He stayed a few minutes and then disappeared.

I lay there until it was dusk, then I moved back closer to the village. I heard faint voices, but the village was getting silent. I waited until I had heard nothing for at least an hour and then moved towards the barrel. When I opened it and reached inside, I was right, it was rice. It had not crossed my mind how I would carry the rice. I remembered in Boy Scouts how we used our pants as a floatation device by tying the legs and filling the pants with air. I thought I could try filling my pants with rice.

Off came my pants, I tied a knot in both legs, zipped the fly and filled the legs with rice. I filled my pants and cinched the waist with my belt. Just as I was finishing, my friend the dog came over. He wagged his tail but whimpered. When he did another dog close by, barked. I grabbed my pants and ran for the stream. I headed upstream but heard no one following me. I stopped for a few minutes to get my breath and then headed back to our little camp.

When I arrived, Tom was awake. As I told him of my escapade, the bombing started again. This time, it was nearer to our area. He thought it was a good sign. He was excited about the food I had brought back.

* * *

The next day, we built a small fire enough to heat water and we boiled the rice. There was not much taste to it, but it was food and we felt fortunate for having it. Later in the day, we heard vehicles coming in our direction. When we heard voices, I said, "I think we need to move. I've left a trail going back and forth to the water. If they see it, they will find us."

Tom agreed and we moved about three hundred yards further upstream. The brush was thicker and the ground more uneven. It would not be as comfortable as our earlier location. However, I hoped we would be safe.

From this vantage point, we had a better view of the wreckage. We had only settled in when we watched several VC, approach it. When they got close, the odor of the bodies was apparent, they looked at each other, said something, and headed in the opposite direction. For the rest of the day, we heard the soldiers. At dusk, we heard the vehicles engines start and leave the area.

* * *

The next day, the heat and humidity were stifling. I was in a daze wondering why no one had been back to rescue us. I was in such deep thought; it took Tom to shake me to recover from my stupor. "Ken, I'm hearing a jet."

"Oh—my—God. Yeah, Tom; I think you are right."

I had Tom take my radio gear and tap out SOS on the microphone. I ran out into the clearing, grabbed a piece of aluminum wreckage, and used the sun to flash the aircraft. It could have been a Chinese MIG. We gambled hoping it would be one of ours.

As I sat out in the opening sending a flash, hoping they could see it. At the altitude they were flying, I was not optimistic. I continued moving the piece hoping for a miracle.

After the jet was out of sight, I returned to where Tom was sitting. I was despondent, "I don't think they saw me."

He said, "Don't say that. Even if they did, they would have to radio back and get instructions."

I asked, "You mean they wouldn't automatically come back?"

I got a half smile from Tom, "Yeah, you would think they would, but we had to wait for Command to approve it. Do not give up hope; they will be back. Maybe you should lie out there and if we hear them again, you can signal."

I returned his smile. "Okay, let's hope you are right."

While waiting, I realized the battery life of my beacon and radio was only a week. Most likely, it would not work even if we tried to call someone. All of sudden we heard the roar of a jet coming our way. I grabbed the metal piece and flashed it in the sun. It did not matter because the jet was flying low enough he should have seen me sitting in the open. I was flashing furiously as he passed overhead. I saw it was an Air Force F-111 and when he made his pass, he tipped his wings twice.

Without thinking and in my excitement, I stood up and screamed, "Tom — He saw us — Tom — He saw us."

I ran back to where Tom was. He reached for me to pull me down. "Ken—Stop screaming. If any VC are in the area, they will hear you. Yeah, I know he saw us."

My actions embarrassed me and I sat next to Tom and apologized. Oh, Shit!" I lowered my voice, "I got so excited. I'm sorry"

Tom laughed, "Yeah, I am too. We have to be patient and careful. The VC might have seen him too."

We waited hoping we would see or hear something showing they were coming to rescue us. When it became sunset, we knew nothing would be happening. After it was dark, we heard aircraft followed by flashes and then rumble of bombs being dropped. By the sound and flashes, it appeared the bombing was closer than previous nights.

We did not move during the night and never talked above a whisper. We kept listening and hoping there would not be any VC coming to our area. We heard nothing. Tom's pain was difficult for him to tolerate and he was running a fever from an infection. I had run out of morphine and I had nothing to give Tom for the pain or the infection. I was using the last bandage on his shoulder wound.

Neither of us slept worrying about the potential for VC. We were convinced someone would be back for us the next day. We were not disappointed.

* * *

It was before noon we heard the roar of a helicopter. As it got closer, I ran back out and grabbed my piece of metal I had used to signal the jet. As I saw it flying about one thousand feet, I furiously flashed my piece of metal. I knew he saw my signal when he made a wide sweep of our area. However, he was not descending.

I ran back to where Tom was sitting, grabbed my flight helmet, put it on, and radioed. "Jolly Green, PJ-2, copy?" I got no response, confirming my batteries were dead.

I was so absorbed in watching what I assumed was our rescue helicopter; I did not see the second one. He came in at one hundred feet in a tight circle and he was on top of me before I saw him.

I grabbed my backpack and said, "Okay Tom, get on. Let's get the hell out." Tom lay across my back and I started out toward the hovering bird. By the time I got to their location, they had lowered the Penetrator. I was out of breath and out of strength from carrying Tom. Somehow, I got Tom and me strapped in. I waved to bird letting them know I was ready. As we were being lifted, the Jolly gained altitude.

As they raised us to the level of the door, I unstrapped and jumped on board. It was then I realized this was my crew and I got excited. Charlie was at the door and I helped him lift Tom onboard and strapped him in a litter.

Once I had Tom secured, I grabbed Charlie, "God — I'm happy to see you guys." He smiled and motioned me to sit. I strapped in a jump seat next to Tom. "You okay?" I yelled. He looked at me and I could see the tears of joy in his eyes. He did not have to say anything.

I plugged my flight helmet into the communication jack and said, "PJ-2, rescue complete, let's go home."

I heard Major Hicks giggle, "PJ-2, Roger that."

Chapter 14

As our Jolly gained altitude, I heard Major Hicks radio, "Jolly four -four, Jolly nine - seven, copy?"

"Jolly nine - seven, 10-4."

"Jolly four - four, you are a go for recovery."

"Jolly nine - seven, Roger that."

I told the Major the locations of the bodies and he passed the information on. Now with the rescue of Colonel Crowley and the recovery of the three KIAs, we could comfortable return knowing, we left no man behind.

* * *

When we landed in Da Nang, over my objection, they forced me to go with Tom to the hospital. I stayed overnight where they gave me fluids, solid food, and rest. Tom had surgery on his leg and placed in a cast. The next day they released me, and before leaving the hospital, I went to see Tom.

As I walked up to his bed in the ward, I said, "Colonel, Sir, how are you feeling?"

Tom gave me a puzzled look, "I'm doing fine. What's this Colonel, Sir, shit?"

I smiled, "If you haven't noticed, we're not in the jungle any longer."

Tom laughed, "I want to thank you for taking care of me."

I interrupted, "I did nothing more than any PJ would have done. The Air Force—"

Tom interrupted, "Bullshit. I know they trained you well. I watched you take control of the situation and you ensured our safety. You took damn, good care of me.

"Thank you, Colonel. As I was saying, the Air Force spent a year training us, and I put the training to good use."

"Doc, I know, but you went beyond it. Now, you let me do my job. I will make sure your exceptional performance is in my report."

"Thank you. Is there anything I can do for you?"

"I don't think so. I have a great nurse taking care of me here. She is a hell of a lot prettier than you." He blushed and burst out laughing.

They sent Tom stateside after two days. I never saw him again. However, the following Christmas, he found me and sent me a Christmas card, thanking me again for taking care of him.

* * *

When I left the hospital, I caught a bus and returned to my barracks. My roommate Tom was out and it felt so odd sitting in my room. Usually, I was tired or intoxicated when I returned and all I wanted to do was crawl into bed. The barracks was not any quieter than any other day. I cannot explain it; I felt out of place. I took a quick shower, changed into fresh fatigues, and walked aimlessly.

There was a library in the NCO Club. While walking, I remembered it had been over a two week since I wrote Genie. I sat in the library at one desk and started my letter. Every time I got a couple sentences written, I tore it up and started again. I wanted to tell her about my last mission, yet I did not want her to worry about me. Most letters, if I told her anything, I lied. Finally, I wrote I missed her and what I wanted to do when I returned to San Antonio.

I don't know how long I had sat, but I was hungry. I decided I would walk to the mess hall. As I headed for the door, Bill Sands was standing in the lobby. When he spotted me, "Hey, Johnson. Where have you been? Everyone is waiting for you."

"What's going on?" I asked.

"Never mind, just follow me."

I followed Bill into the main bar area of the club. When my eyes adapted to the dim lighting, I spotted two large tables with at least 20 men, including eight PJs from our squadron. As I walked up, I realized everyone from my team was present. Someone had put together a party to celebrate the successful completion of our mission and my return.

It was the first time since I had joined Detachment 7 I felt part of the group and not an outsider. I had PJs speaking whom never spoke other than a greeting. I had officers besides Major Hicks and Captain Blair come over and congratulate me on a successful mission. I was uncomfortable being the center of attention. However, after my second drink, I let go of my defenses and enjoyed the party. During the evening, and after too many drinks, I announced, "Hey guys, I've got one month, twenty days and a wake-up."

* * *

The colonel gave our team a full rotation or three days off. However, after the second day, they called us back in. There were six birds on missions and no one but us was left. Before the day was over, we flew a backup mission. The recovery was for one of our squadron's Jolly, which took an artillery hit.

They had ditched the Jolly in the South China Sea with no serious injuries to the crew. It was my first experience of a rescue in water since Pipeline training. They equipped the lead and our bird with pontoons on each side of the aircraft. From our standby position, I watched as the lead bird first hovered and then lowered itself into the water to recover the crew from a life raft. It was an impressive recovery.

* * *

It was two weeks after our mission to recover Colonel Crowley when I checked in for my crew's standby status; Colonel Price called me his office. Walking down the hall, I was asking myself, what now?"

When I walked in, Major Hicks and Captain Blair were standing next to the Colonel's desk. As I entered, Colonel Price smiled, "Sergeant Johnson, please come in." I saluted the Colonel. "At ease, please take a seat."

Major Hicks and Captain Blair sat with me while Colonel Price read a memo from Air Combat Command 23rd Air Force Headquarters. The first part was recognizing the 38th ARRS squadron for its outstanding performance. It mentioned outstanding performances by Detachment 7, 9, and other units. Then it detailed the mission in November 1969 where Major Hicks and Captain Blair had performed heroically in saving their aircraft and crew after being hit by enemy fire. It listed the outstanding and heroic performance of Pararescue Sergeant Ken Johnson when left behind enemy lines and saved the life of Lieutenant Colonel Thomas Crowley. It concluded by recommending the award to Major Hicks and his crew the Meritorious Service Medal for our outstanding service. It further recommended the award to Detachment 7 of the 38th ARRS the Joint Meritorious Unit Award.

When he finished, Colonel Price was beaming. When he walked around his desk, the three of us jumped up to attention. Colonel Price said, "At ease Gentlemen, at ease." He congratulated and thanked each one of us and shook our hands. He paused and looking directly at me, he said, "Sergeant Johnson, if I have anything to say about it, you should receive a Bronze Star for your heroism."

I couldn't believe what I was hearing. Was he talking about me, the guy he was ready to boot out a few weeks ago. I was speechless, all I could say was, "Thank you, Sir."

Two weeks later, in a ceremony with the majority of Detachment 7 in attendance, Major Hicks, Captain Blair, Technical Sergeant Kiesler, Sergeant Sands and myself received the Meritorious Service Medal. The colonel announced Detachment 7 was receiving the Joint Meritorious Unit Award. Major Hicks threw us a party at the Officer's Club that night. From the day they recognized me for my achievement in Colonel Price's office until I left the military, I never again felt inferior among my PJ peers.

The mission was declassified where I spent those 10 days in the jungle with Colonel Crowley; we were fifty miles north of the DMZ in North Vietnam. Due to the heavy enemy activity and especially a SAM site within miles of our location, command disallowed a recovery mission. Once they took out the SAM site and the grounds troops scattered, they allowed Major Hicks to return.

* * *

January 10, 1970, I left Da Nang heading home. My return flight was by Air Force aircraft as opposed to the commercial one when I came over a year prior. I caught a flight to Clark AFB in the Philippines. I sat in a cold hanger with twenty or more men waiting for space on the next flight heading out.

Captain Blair left a day after I did. He used his influence as an officer, to get himself and me on the next flight. I felt guilty because there were men waiting longer than I did. After a short layover at Hickam AFB in Hawaii, I arrived at Travis AFB in California.

When I got to Travis, they held me over. They told me because of my security level, they needed to debrief me. "Debrief for what?" I asked. I spent four hours listening to them tell me what I could say and what I could not. I didn't know any security stuff. We had been in Laos and Cambodia when the President said we were not.

What I knew of the war was the long tedious hours every day with little or no relief. My personal experience was the day after day of missions where we put our lives at risk, hoping to rescue some poor sap who was shot down or their aircraft malfunctioned. Each time we flew in, we hoped we found them alive and did not have to return with the horrid black bag. What I knew of the war was seeing the tremendous number of wounded and dead men. I wanted to get home and somehow forget where I had been and what I had seen.

They gave me a physical before I left Travis. The doctor came in, "Sergeant Johnson, you have tested positive for marijuana."

By this time, I did not give a shit and cockily replied, "So what, I'm sure I'm not the first." Because of his report, they searched my duffle bag. I somehow had the forethought to give what little marijuana I had to someone in my barracks before I left.

* * *

After a week since I had left Vietnam, I arrived in San Antonio. Paul drove Genie to the airport, and as I stepped into the terminal, she was in my arms crying. "I thought this day would never come," she sobbed. "Please promise me you will never leave me again."

I handed her my handkerchief and she dried her face. "I told you when you left I would not be okay until you returned. I love you, but please, promise me you will never do this again." I pulled her into my arms and told her what she wanted to hear.

Genie gave me a few days to rest, and then the following Saturday night, threw a party to celebrate my return. She rented the clubhouse at the apartment complex and many of the friends who attended our wedding came.

* * *

The following week, we went to Ft. Worth to see my parents. My dad said they tried several times to visit Genie, but each time they attempted, she gave an excuse it was inconvenient. He said they only saw her during the Christmas holidays. It only confirmed Genie had suffered while I was away and it only added to my guilt.

After leaving Ft. Worth, I fulfilled a promise I had made in Vietnam. We drove to Houston and the home of Jimmy's parents. I first called them to make sure they would be home. I had their address, and when we drove into their neighborhood, I could not believe what I was seeing.

Jimmy never once had said his family was wealthy. As we drove down his parent's street, looking for their address, we passed one mansion after another. It was an older neighborhood, although, the homes were immaculate. When we found the house, it was a two-story brick with large white pillars accenting the colonial styling. I parked in their circular driveway.

I dressed in my Class A Blues, with my jump boots, beret, medals, and all. I think I wanted to give homage to their son and show how proud Jimmy was to be a PJ. For me, it was another way to honor his heroic death and my friendship.

As soon as we got out of the car, the front door opened and his parent stepped out. His parents warmly welcomed Genie and I and ushered us into their home. To our surprise, not only did his parents welcome us; they had invited close friends and family for the reception. They introduced me as Jimmy's best friend and military comrade.

After a respectable time, while hors d'oeuvres and drinks were served, I told Jimmy's parents I had something I wanted to present to them. The room went quiet, Genie handed me the box and I lifted the beret with the flash. I had taken his jump and flight wings and pinned them to the top.

I said, "Mr. and Mrs. Douglas, Jimmy belonged to the elite Thirty-Eighth Aeronautical Rescue and Recovery Squadron. I wanted to honor his memory by returning his beret and flash to you. Not only was he a special friend he was a hero to everyone who knew him."

After handing Jimmy's beret to his mother, I stepped back, came to attention, and then gave a salute. I knew the tears would come, but I prepared myself. What I didn't want was lose it in front of everyone. I kept my composure without embarrassment.

Before we left, we got direction to the cemetery. Genie held my hand as I stood in front of Jimmy's grave. What I had kept inside for so many months; came flooding out. Once I recovered, I once again, came to attention, saluted, and walked away. I thought it was my final tribute to my best friend.

***

Genie had made Buck Sergeant (E-4) before I returned. They promoted me to Staff Sergeant (E-5) just before I left Da

Nang. When I returned to work, they again assigned me to Wilford Hall and worked in the emergency room and surgery. It had been six months since I worked in surgery and I felt rusty. What really felt great, after working eight hours I could go home.

After being acclimated to regular duty, Personnel started their campaign to persuade me to reenlist. Even when I was adamant I was not interested, they continued to have me meet with different individuals attempting to make me change my mind. I had met several PJs who decided to reenlist only to regret it. However, I admit there were those career-oriented individuals who did decide to reenlist. I always wondered if they knew something, I did not or were they 'gung-ho'. I did talk to my dad. He had spent over 33 years in the Air Force and I wanted to hear his advice. He said, "The Air Force is not the same as it was in my earlier career. It is more political and promotions were no longer based on merit; it is whom you know. Commanders don't have the latitude to decide those issues that affect the individual and their families." His list of negative reasons far exceeded his positive.

My experience had taught me PJs made rank quickly; it exceeded the normal NCO. However, because of their expertise, they earned their promotions by working in the dangerous and risk-taking environment. It was no secret, as long as the Vietnam War continued, any PJ who reenlisted they sent back for a second and sometimes a third deployment. In my mind, there was no promotion, no enlistment bonus, or future promise substantial enough to get me to return to Vietnam. All I wanted was to finish my enlistment and get out.

Starting in 1968, the military offered early discharge for individuals not reenlisting and were accepted at an accredited college, university, or trade school. Knowing this, I enrolled at San Antonio Community College in February 1970 going to classes in the evening. I applied for early termination, and in March of 1970, I was honorably discharged from the Air Force. Wives on active duty were discharged and Genie was released one week later.

Conclusion

I was discharged from the Air Force for more than a year, when I got a letter from the Air Force, informing me they awarded me the Bronze Star for my act of heroism of November 1969. It gave me instructions to contact the Air Force. When they had their next award ceremony, they would award me the metal.

I was in college and had no desire to re-associate myself with the Air Force. I had become bitter towards the military and the political system, which had sent me to Vietnam. I suffered nightmares from the horrors I experienced. I spent sleepless nights seeing the faces of those killed and injured by this needless war. I felt guilty for those I treated, who later died because I could not do more. I wanted all those memories to disappear. No—I did not give a damn about any medal.

*　*　*

It was twenty-something years later when in Washington D.C., I visited the Vietnam Memorial and again faced Jimmy's name along with thousands more being honored at the 'Wall'. The day I stood there in front of the memorial, I wondered how so many could have died for a war, which brought nothing but dishonor to our nation. How would our families, friends, and our nation ever heal?

* * *

It has been over 45 years since I returned from Vietnam. Most of these years, I did not acknowledge I was a Vietnam Veteran. If asked, I would admit I was in the Air Force, but rarely told anyone what I did. I was not ashamed; however, thinking about it brought back all those nightmares. Being a Vietnam Veteran during those years was nothing honorable. If you met another veteran, you might share war stories while sharing a beer.

Today, the public sentiment has changed. We are recognizing the Veterans of the Mid-East Wars for their valor and sacrifices. There is an outcry for reform when we spot abuse of veterans' rights or discrimination. Post Traumatic Stress Disorder (PTSD) is not anything new. The symptoms now have a name and acknowledge as a real side effect of war experiences. Veterans of previous wars also suffered from PTSD, although, it was not discussed or treated. It was previously a weakness.

For the Vietnam Veteran, the change in public attitude has its good and bad effect. It's positive after all these years the Vietnam Veteran is being recognized. It is way overdue, for heroes both living and dead; we give them their honorable place in history. There are thousands of individuals have hid in the shadows of fear and shame. It is the time we revered them.

For the Vietnam Veteran, to come out of those shadows, they have to face those fears, and self-doubts they have kept hidden. There were things done for personal survival or sanity if enlightened would not bring honor. There are the personal losses, disabling injuries, and mental traumas, which they have healed and forgotten. To acknowledge our courage includes bringing to light all those things we have wanted to forget.

I cannot speak for all Vietnam Veterans; being recognized for serving my country at a time of war, returns the lost self-pride. I only wish those symbols of heroism I earned; I would have cherished and protected them. My beret with its Pararescue Flash, my jump wings, flight crew wings along with my ribbons, and medals were lost. For years, I kept a uniform in the back of my closet, only to dispose of it.

I am following many writers who have taken their suppressed memories and nightmares and placed them into print. I took the challenge and filled those blank pages with the experiences of training and serving proudly as a PJ. Whether my writing is of value to the reader, it will be determined later. However, what it has done for my self-esteem and mental perception is a value, no one can judge as wrong. I will always believe in the PJ motto.

"These things we do, so others may live."

Made in the USA
San Bernardino, CA
17 March 2018